THE HIDDEN WORLD OF
Changers

No.5: The Shadow Fox

by H. K. Varian

Simon Spotlight

New York London Toronto Sydney New Delhi

This book is a work of fiction. Any references to historical events, real people, or real places are used fictitiously. Other names, characters, places, and events are products of the author's imagination, and any resemblance to actual events or places or persons, living or dead, is entirely coincidental.

SIMON SPOTLIGHT
An imprint of Simon & Schuster Children's Publishing Division
1230 Avenue of the Americas, New York, New York 10020
This Simon Spotlight paperback edition January 2017
Copyright © 2017 by Simon & Schuster, Inc.
Text by Laurie Calkhoven
Illustrations by Tony Foti
All rights reserved, including the right of reproduction in whole or in part in any form.
SIMON SPOTLIGHT and colophon are registered trademarks of Simon & Schuster, Inc.
For information about special discounts for bulk purchases, please contact Simon & Schuster Special Sales at 1-866-506-1949 or business@simonandschuster.com.
Designed by Nick Sciacca
The text of this book was set in Celestia Antiqua.
Manufactured in the United States of America 1216 OFF
10 9 8 7 6 5 4 3 2 1
ISBN 978-1-4814-8082-6 (hc)
ISBN 978-1-4814-8081-9 (pbk)
ISBN 978-1-4814-8083-3 (eBook)
Library of Congress Catalog Card Number 2016939209

Kitsune

...e of the most powerful Changers. ...om the Far East, this massive fox ...eature possesses many incredible ...ilities, including commanding fire ...d creating illusions.

...fur is typically red, and its paws ... engulfed in flame, though they ...er burn. Kitsunes can have as many ...nine tails, which they collect ...roughout their lifetime by ...quiring knowledge or ...complishing heroic deeds. ...e more tails a kitsune ...s, the more ...werful ...ecomes.

Nine-tailed kitsunes possess incredible powers, including the ability to see anything happening anywhere in the world. Upon acquiring its ninth tail, the kitsune's fur turns white.

PROLOGUE

Mack filled the teakettle and set it on the stove, carefully measuring green tea into his *jiichan's*, or grandfather's, Japanese teapot. Then he began to tidy up the living room to get ready for this morning's gathering.

Life had been a whirlwind ever since the first day of seventh grade, when Makoto "Mack" Kimura had been told that he was a Changer—someone descended from a line of magical shape-shifters who had been forgotten by history. Changers can transform into different magical creatures that hold incredible power. To ordinary people, Changers are mythological animals that only exist in the pages of fantasy books, but Mack had learned that they were real.

In his Changer form—a *kitsune*—Mack became a massive fox whose paws blazed with fire. He had two tails and could earn even more by learning new abilities and completing heroic deeds. Mack was still a long way from mastering his powers, but luckily, he wasn't alone. Three of his classmates were also Changers, and together, they were being trained to use their powers to protect both human- and Changer-kind alike from powerful witches and warlocks who sought to control the world with dark magic.

Mack's classmate Fiona Murphy had learned she was a *selkie*, a seal, with a repertoire of magical songs that were incredibly powerful. Gabriella Rivera, a *nahual*, could transform into a powerful black jaguar; she was practically unbeatable in a fight and had a cool spirit-walking ability to boot. And *impundulu* Darren Smith could become a huge bird with the power to channel lightning and summon storms.

The seventh graders were being trained by the First Four, a group of Changers who had led the Changer nation for the last thousand years. Mack's grandfather, Akira Kimura, was part of the First Four.

Mack's grandfather was a *kitsune* like Mack; he'd earned nine tails throughout his very long life, the most tails a *kitsune* can earn. Dorina Therian, a werewolf, was the seventh graders' main teacher and led a Changer class in the secretly enchanted gym at Willow Cove Middle School. Yara Moreno, an *encantado*, or dolphin Changer, was often away on missions, but Mack liked having her around. Yara trusted Mack and his friends, and their abilities, more than any other member of the First Four—she never treated them like little kids. On the other hand, Sefu Badawi, a *bultungin*, or hyena Changer, was Yara's polar opposite. His role in the Changer nation was to protect Changers from outside threats, and sometimes he could be a bit, well, *overprotective.*

Together, the First Four steered Mack, Gabriella, Darren, and Fiona in the discovery and control of their new powers. And they were all coming for this morning's meeting.

Mack fluffed couch pillows, folded newspapers for the recycling bin, and shook his head thinking about how steep his learning curve had been ever since he got the news in September. Powers begin to develop in a Changer's twelfth year, and he had learned what he was just before that started to happen. The first day of school immersed Mack and his friends in a new, secret, and sometimes confusing world.

Changers, witches, and warlocks weren't always hidden away. They used to live openly alongside normal humans, bringing rain for crops, protecting villages, and healing the sick. But a thousand years ago, a warlock used a magical horn, the Horn of Power, to force Changers to do his bidding. Many people were hurt; entire villages destroyed. Even after the First Four put an end to the warlock and took away the horn, non-magical people believed that Changers were dangerous. They turned on the Changers, hunting them down until the Changers had been forced to go into hiding. Despite everything, Changers continued to do what they could to protect mankind, but now they had to do it in secret.

Just as Mack, Gabriella, Darren, and Fiona were starting to learn how to handle their powers, a new warlock, Auden Ironbound, stole the Horn of Power and tried to recreate the terrible events that had transpired a thousand years ago. When Auden used the horn to take control of the First Four, it fell upon Mack and his friends to battle the warlock and his army on their own. Under the cover of a massive, magical storm, Mack himself had fought and defeated Auden on the beach of their small town, Willow Cove. Mack had even damaged the Horn of Power.

As the Changers soon discovered, though, Auden was down but not out. Mack and his friends clashed with Auden's henchmen as they sought out a magical artifact, Circe's Compass, which Auden could use to find younglings, or Changers who hadn't yet come of age. Auden needed the magic of five different younglings to mend the Horn of Power. Once the horn was repaired and Auden rounded up another army to march on Willow Cove, all hope seemed lost. But once again, the Changers pulled through, thanks in part to Fiona, who had learned a magical *selkie* song that stripped the evil warlock of his magic once and for all and destroyed the Horn of Power for good.

But perhaps even more shocking than their sudden victory a few months ago was a secret that had been revealed to them just before the battle: hundreds of years ago, Mack, Gabriella, Darren, and Fiona had been foretold to be the next leaders of Changer-kind. It wasn't chance that the four of them lived in the same small town of Willow Cove—a town that was home to an important Changer base. It was also why the First Four took such an interest in Mack and his friends and why they were training them personally . . . and why Mack was so impatient for more information.

After several long months of waiting, today—finally—the First Four planned to tell Mack and his friends more about the prophecy and what it meant for their training and their futures.

Mack finished tidying up the living room and sought out his grandfather. He found Jiichan meditating in his office. Hearing Mack's footsteps, Jiichan opened his eyes and then smiled.

"Is everything ready, Makoto?" he asked.

"Almost," Mack said. "I just have to shovel the walk. . . ." In truth, something had been weighing heavily on Mack these last few months, ever since his last battle. Something *other* than the prophecy, but he wasn't sure if now was the best time to broach the subject with Jiichan again.

"I know the wait has been difficult for you," Jiichan began, sensing that Mack was holding something back. "But the time wasn't right to reveal the prophecy. You needed more training before beginning the next phase of your journey—"

"There's actually, um, something else that's been bothering me, Jiichan," Mack cut in. "Remember a few months ago, after the battle with Auden, how I saw a golden *kitsune* on the battlefield, with seven tails? I've been wondering about her. I know Sefu said she used to be your student—"

Jiichan cut off Mack midquestion. "I've told you already that I will not discuss this, Makoto. I have lived a very long life, and made my share of mistakes. Not every memory I have is a happy one. There are some things that I simply choose not to dwell on. I'd prefer we not discuss this further."

Mack clenched his teeth. Jiichan could be so mysterious when he wanted to be. Mack knew that Changers lived much longer than non-magical people—that Jiichan was at least a thousand years old—but what could be so bad that his grandfather wouldn't even talk about it? Based on the First Four's reaction to the golden *kitsune*, he knew that she was important and possibly dangerous—too dangerous to be ignored.

Wouldn't it be better to clue Mack and the others in on the threat? They'd proven themselves more than capable of dealing with the Changers' enemies. Sure, they lacked experience, but Mack felt like his grandfather was always underestimating them.

Mack took a breath, ready to press the matter.

Jiichan interrupted again. "This is not a story I want to tell. Not now."

"But—"

"Leave it alone, Makoto." Jiichan's tone was frighteningly final. Mack rarely ever heard his calm *jiichan* raise his voice.

Mack quickly realized any further argument was useless. It was no secret that he and Jiichan were alike in more than just their Changer ability—they could both be stubborn and prideful. With nothing else to say, Mack trudged to the kitchen and lit the fire under the teakettle before heading outside to shovel snow.

Will the time ever be right to tell me everything? Mack seethed.

More and more it had been bothering Mack how little the First Four revealed to him and his friends about the wider Changer world. It seemed like they divulged one little secret at a time, and even those secrets hid more secrets.

Secrets within secrets within secrets. I'm tired of being kept in the dark. Will they ever tell us the whole truth?

Just then, a flash of light in the corner of Mack's eye caught his attention. He looked up and saw a streak of gold bolting across the tree-lined field in the distance.

Was that—? Mack thought as he started to walk forward to get a better look.

"Mack!" Gabriella called out a car window, jolting Mack from his thoughts. An SUV pulled into the drive. Gabriella and Darren climbed out of the backseat, followed by Ms. Therian and Sefu from the front.

Mack looked into the distance again. He was *almost* sure . . . the golden *kitsune* . . .

But whatever he saw, it was gone.

Chapter 1
The Prophecy

Mack led the group into the living room just as Jiichan was emerging from the kitchen, carrying the teapot and eight porcelain teacups on an antique tray.

A moment later Fiona and Yara, the two waterborne Changers, arrived together.

Fiona looked in Mack's direction and raised her eyebrows. *Did you learn anything else about the golden kitsune?* she thought to him. Another useful ability Changers had was being able to speak telepathically to each other. It came in handy when they were all in their animal forms and speaking English, or even just speaking out loud, wasn't exactly an option.

For the last few months, Fiona had tried to help Mack find more information about the golden *kitsune* in an ancient book of Changer history known as *The Compendium*. It had family trees, the locations of Changer bases, and detailed accounts of Changer battles, but the book only allowed certain people to read certain pages. It never really gave you the whole picture, much like the First Four.

Nothing yet, Mack thought back, still feeling frustrated.

Fiona gave him a sympathetic smile and joined the group around the coffee table, where Jiichan was carefully pouring tea for each of them.

Mack and his friends had waited a long time for this day. Fiona's eyes sparkled with curiosity while Gabriella, a superathlete in both her human and Changer forms, was ready to leap into action and do whatever needed to be done. Even Darren, who'd had doubts about his new Changer life, waited a little impatiently to hear what the First Four had to say.

The First Four exchanged pleasantries about the weather and sipped their tea. It was all Mack could do not to shout, *Spill it already! Tell us about the prophecy*, but he knew that would only slow everything down *and* upset his grandfather.

Ms. Therian caught Jiichan's eye and nodded. "It's time, Akira," she said.

"Before we begin," Jiichan addressed Mack, Gabriella, Darren, and Fiona, "I want to be sure that each of you is ready. Once you embark upon this path, there is no turning back. You'll be more than Changers; you'll be leaders in training. That's not something you can walk away from. It's also something we'd hoped to delay for a few more years, but as Yara would say—"

"The cat's out of the bag," Yara finished.

In the tense silence that followed, Jiichan's dark eyes took in each of the younglings, one at a time. Fiona nodded solemnly, as did Gabriella. Darren hesitated and then did the same.

"I'm ready," Mack said. "No turning back."

Ms. Therian stood and carefully reached into her satchel, pulling out an exquisitely carved box made of silver maple. Mack recognized it immediately. It was the box that held the Changing Stone—the stone that had revealed their Changer abilities to them on the first day of school.

There was total silence as she lifted the box's lid and removed the large, round moonstone from the folds of midnight-blue silk. Mack remembered that it had been forged by magic thousands of years ago. A non-magical person looking at it would simply see a beautiful gemstone, milky-white streaked with color, like a giant opal. But when a Changer gazed into it, the stone revealed his or her true form.

But they knew all about their Changer forms now. . . . Why did they need the stone again? "We already know—" Mack blurted.

Ms. Therian's eyes on his were enough to make him be quiet. *More waiting,* he thought.

"Stand with me and put your hands on the stone," she said. "All together."

Mack, Fiona, Darren, and Gabriella did as she asked. Then the First Four filled the spaces in between them and started to do the same. The whole thing was a little awkward, almost like a team huddle. But as soon as Jiichan, the last of them, placed his fingers on the stone, it began to emit a shimmering light that pulsed and quivered. The magic drew him in, until Mack could feel the room around him falling away. All was dark. It was as though Mack had been transported somewhere else.

What is this? Mack wondered. Even though he couldn't see anyone else, he thought he could still sense the presence of the others nearby. *Where on Earth are we?*

Mack's thoughts were interrupted by the sight of a beautiful and ethereal woman, stepping out of the darkness. Her white robes fluttered against her dark skin as her long coiled hair swirled. Then, with a flick of her wrist, a scene began to materialize around him. That's when Mack noticed her eyes—bright amber eyes that seemed to hold all the peace and joy and magic in the world.

Mack barely had time to wonder who she was when many voices began to talk in unison. Without anyone telling him, Mack knew in his heart that the voices were those of every Changer leader who had ever lived, speaking as one.

"In the beginning, when mankind was in its infancy, there was a woman named Circe. Circe wasn't like other humans. She could see and feel the magic that flowed through our world, and harness it. She used her magic to do good, creating abundance and prosperity for all who knew her."

Mack watched as the woman he guessed was Circe calmed the stormy waters of the ocean, saved villagers from a mudslide, stopped a war, and healed the sick. Everywhere she went, it seemed, peace and happiness blossomed.

"As time passed, Circe found that she didn't age like other humans did. In fact, she didn't seem to age at all. Her gifts became stronger with time, and she decided to awaken those gifts in others. She took on five apprentices and taught them how to wield magic, but one of them, a girl named Morwyn, was the most powerful."

Mack watched as the five apprentices joined hands with Circe, and then one—Morwyn—stepped into the center of the circle. Morwyn had bright eyes, similar to Circe, but somehow, this feature didn't instill the same peace in Mack as Circe had. Morwyn's eyes were also angry and defiant. Mack felt a shiver of uneasiness creep up his spine.

After a brief pause, the voices continued.

"When they were ready, the five apprentices moved throughout the world. Four of them used their magical abilities for good, as Circe had. But Morwyn was different.

"Morwyn didn't want to use her magic for the benefit of mankind; instead she used her magic to inflict pain and turn normal humans, whom she believed to be inferior, into her servants."

Mack watched a trail of people stumble across a hot desert, following Morwyn. Their expressions—sad and frightened—made Mack want to turn away from the scene.

The Changer leaders continued their story. "When Morwyn's fellow apprentices heard tales of the terror she had wrought, they threw themselves at Circe's feet and begged her to make them stronger so that they could defeat Morwyn. But Circe knew that to defeat Morwyn, normal magic wouldn't be enough. So Circe dug deeper, and awoke in her four apprentices something greater—a magic that was transformative—Changer magic."

Mack watched with amazement as the four

apprentices transformed—one into a *kitsune* like him, another into a spider, and the last two into a bear and a sea serpent, respectively.

"With this new power the apprentices became the first Changers. They took on animal forms and defeated Morwyn, but Circe found she could not let them harm her prodigy. Rather, the dark apprentice was banished to the north."

Mack observed as Morwyn, still defiant, walked away from the others, ultimately disappearing into a mist. Behind her he saw another long trail of followers. These people were not the same sad and powerless lot that he had seen earlier. These beings had an anger and malice that nearly matched Morwyn's.

"In her exile, Morwyn found many followers who became the witches and warlocks we know today."

Mack watched Morwyn's followers form a circle around her. As if there was a movie camera pulling back for a wide shot, the circle got bigger and bigger and bigger as more witches and warlocks joined Morwyn. He shivered at their overwhelming number as the leaders continued the story.

"Meanwhile, Circe awakened the Changer ability in anyone she met who was in need of magic, and some of them passed that ability to their children, and so on. From the original Changer apprentices, the First Four, the Changers soon grew into millions."

The vision pulsed again, and the Changers, Mack saw, quickly outnumbered the witches and warlocks.

"The Changers needed strong leaders," the voices said. "The First Four apprentices stepped up to the task, and that title has been passed down to new leaders through the millennia. The First Four keep Changers focused on their sacred mission to guard and protect mankind, as Circe has done. Every so often, four new leaders are foretold, trained, and protected until they come of age."

Mack saw a vision of himself and his friends on the first day of seventh grade, each staring in awe at the Changing Stone.

"Today a new age draws breath, one of peace between Changer- and magic-kind. Four younglings shall bear the banners of change. . . .

"The last of a powerful bloodline."

Mack watched as the image morphed. He caught a brief glimpse of his older self as he Changed into a nine-tailed *kitsune*. His fur was white, like Jiichan's, and the flames that licked at his paws were blazingly hot. He thought for a moment about the other seven tails he still had to earn. What would he accomplish in the future to win them?

"The heir of a wayward hero," the voices said next.

Mack's older *kitsune* form dissolved, and he saw Gabriella, now an adult, standing on a rooftop wearing what looked like the Emerald Wildcat's outfit as she looked down over a nighttime city. Gabriella's aunt Rosa was also a *nahual*, and she had once used her powers to fight crime in New Brighton as a superhero called the Emerald Wildcat. Is *this Gabriella's fate too?* Mack wondered as the older Gabriella Changed into her black jaguar form and leaped into the streets below.

"The storm-born son of an ancient power."

Mack next saw a shadow of Darren, who was now much taller and broader in the shoulders. Darren was stooping to pull up a group of people, one by one, from below. As he helped them up, each changed into a bird and took flight. Finally, there was a crack of thunder, and Darren Changed too. Mack could feel gale-force winds on his face as Darren took to the skies, thunder booming overhead.

And lastly, the voices rang out once more. "The hidden daughter of a conflicted queen."

A grown-up Fiona stood on a rocky shore, wearing a crown of coral and pearls, her red hair bright against her gray *selkie* cloak. She was leading hooded figures out of the ocean and onto the beach. She embraced several of them before transforming and diving back into the ocean, her sleek *selkie* pelt glistening in the sunshine.

A final vision formed. The older Mack, Gabriella, Darren, and Fiona stood strong together, looking ready to face anything. And then suddenly, Mack was back in his living room, and the light of the moonstone had faded beneath his hand.

Chapter 2
The Next Step

The first thing Darren noticed was the incredulous looks on his friends' faces. Darren didn't know what to expect from today's meeting, but he was pretty sure no one could've guessed it would be *that*. Fiona was looking up at the First Four with new appreciation. Mack and Gabriella smiled at Ms. Therian with the same slightly awed expression.

"It's our duty to guide you as we were once guided long ago," Ms. Therian said.

Yara, her face wreathed in wrinkles as she beamed at them, said, "You've met and exceeded all our expectations so far."

"We're very proud," Sefu added.

Darren looked at Mr. Kimura and saw pride in his eyes as well.

"There are many special abilities that come with being the First Four, abilities that you will learn when you're ready," he said.

Beside Darren, Mack tried unsuccessfully to suppress a groan. Darren felt his pain—he too was tired of all the secrets.

Mack's grandfather reached out to put a hand on Mack's shoulder. "You all must trust that we know what's best for your training."

Before Mack had time to respond, Fiona raised her hand.

"Yes, Fiona," Mr. Kimura said gently.

"I have a few questions. Who makes the prophecies? Who decided that we"—she gestured to the rest of the kids—"are leaders? And how do they know for sure?"

"Circe makes the prophecies," Ms. Therian said. "She's now very, very old, of course, but her connection to this world's magic is stronger than ever. Circe's Order delivers the prophecies to us, the current First Four, and we in turn use them to guide the Changer nation."

"Circe's Order?" Mack repeated. "What is that? Who's in it?"

"The order is very secretive, and its members are chosen by Circe," Sefu answered. "It's comprised of Changer- and magic-kind alike. Those who have chosen the path of Circe over Morwyn's."

"You mean there are *good* magic-users out there?" Gabriella asked.

Yara laughed, although Darren didn't see why. So far, all the magic-users he had come up against were dangerous and evil.

"Of course there are," Yara said. "They live much quieter lives than the witches and warlocks you've encountered. But they're there, in the shadows, secretly doing good."

"For that matter," Sefu added ominously, "there are bad Changers out there, too."

Mack nodded. "Like the dolphin that tried to steal Circe's Compass from Fiona."

Darren cringed. In their search for the compass, Darren and the others had led an *encantado* working for

Auden Ironbound right to it. The kids, with the help of the First Four, had only just managed to keep it out of the hands of the warlock's followers.

"Did Circe make the compass?" Fiona asked. "Is that why it has her name?"

"Circe created several powerful relics. The compass is just one of them," Sefu confirmed.

Darren knew Fiona was about to ask for a history of every relic ever created. Before he had to listen to another long story, he jumped in with a question of his own. "So what now?" he asked. "What's next?"

Ms. Therian smiled at the four of them. "To lead our people, you have to know them," she said. "Now that you know your destiny, it's time you learned more about the Changers' world."

"How do we do that?" Darren asked. "It's not like I can just walk up to someone on the street and say, 'Hey, can you change into a magical creature? I'm a giant lightning bird.'"

"We'll begin with a field trip," she answered, her eyes dancing with mischief. "To Wyndemere Academy, the only boarding school in America just for Changers."

Darren hadn't expected that. He stood quietly and watched as Fiona, Gabriella, and Mack babbled questions about Wyndemere Academy. Fiona was so excited she didn't even raise her hand.

"A boarding school just for Changers?" she asked. "Where is it? What kinds of special classes do they offer?"

At the same time, Gabriella was asking about the school's sports teams. Darren could tell by the way she was flexing her muscles that she was ready to compete against other Changers on the athletic field. And Mack wanted to know all about the types of Changers they hadn't seen yet.

Werewolves and selkies *aren't enough?* Darren wondered.

"You'll have to get permission from your parents," Ms. Therian said, pulling two packets of papers out of her bag.

"Now that my father knows I'm a *selkie*, I know he'll say yes," Fiona said. "He says yes to anything involving education."

Darren's heart sank. Like Fiona's dad, Darren's mom

was a professor at New Brighton University and valued education. But she didn't know that Darren was a Changer, and there were other complicated reasons she might say no.

Ms. Therian handed the packets of information to Gabriella and Darren. "These are for your parents," she said.

Darren looked at the cover. The title *National Park Nature Trip* was printed over a picture of Olympic National Park.

"Your mother, Gabriella, and your parents, Darren, will think that's where you're going," she said, pointing to the picture. "Our real destination is Wyndemere Academy."

"I'm sure my mom will say yes, but Tía Rosa can convince her even if she doesn't," Gabriella put in.

"There's a Changer school right out in the open?" Mack asked, looking over Gabriella's shoulder.

"It's hidden away on ocean cliffs, not far from the national park," Ms. Therian said, "and protected by enchantments."

"When do we leave?" Gabriella asked.

"In three weeks," Mr. Kimura said. "We want to stay under the radar as much as possible, so your trip will be over Willow Cove Middle School's spring break, leaving on Thursday and returning on Sunday."

"You'll need every minute between now and then to train for the Youngling Games," Yara said with a mischievous smile.

"Games?" Gabriella piped up.

Darren knew that sports and competition were totally Gabriella's jam. He was a pretty good athlete himself and played on Willow Cove's football team, but Gabriella dominated every sport she played, and that was *before* she developed her *nahual* powers. Now her *nahual* abilities made her unstoppable.

"Games," Ms. Therian said with a nod. "The Youngling Games are a series of sporting events that Changers aged eleven to thirteen from all over the country come to Wyndemere Academy to compete in."

Gabriella was bouncing on her toes. Darren thought she might change into her *nahual* form out of sheer excitement. "Can we sign up for multiple events?"

"And can I *not* sign up for any of Gabriella's races?"

Mack asked. "I'm not sure I can take losing over and over again."

Ms. Therian laughed heartily. "Yes, you can—both of you," she said to Mack and Gabriella. Then her eyes swept the four of them. "There are different events for all of you."

"All of us?" Fiona asked, her forehead wrinkled with concern. "Athletics aren't really my thing. Can't I write a history of the games instead of competing?"

Everyone laughed. Fiona was the only kid they knew who *enjoyed* writing research papers. She took every advanced class Willow Cove Middle School had to offer and aced them all.

"There are water events for *selkies*, *encantados*, and the other waterborne Changers," Yara said. "You'll have fun." Then she turned to Darren. "You've been awfully quiet, Darren. Aren't you excited about meeting other *impundulus*?"

Everyone turned to look at him, and Darren cringed. "Sure I am," he said, but his heart wasn't in it.

"Is something wrong?" Gabriella asked gently.

Darren was about to brush off the question, but he

knew she and Fiona would keep asking until he told them what was really going on. He wanted to go to Wyndemere Academy, but it wasn't that easy, especially when his parents were in the middle of getting divorced.

"I don't think my mom will let me go," he said finally. "My parents agreed to shared custody—I'll be living mostly with my mom. I don't have to go to court or anything, but I do have to go to a few counseling sessions with a therapist. The sessions are coming up soon, and the counselor decides if it's okay for me to live with my mom or not. . . ." His voice trailed off. He hated to think about sitting in a room for hours while some stranger decided which parent he would live with. At least his big brother, Ray, who had already left home for New Brighton University, would be home in a few weeks to help him get through it. His Changer friends had been really nice about everything, too.

Mr. Kimura smiled reassuringly at Darren. "I think your mother would like you to get away for a while," he said. "She's been worried about you since the divorce was announced."

Darren remembered the family meeting his parents

had a few months ago with him and Ray. He'd nearly lost control of his lightning abilities trying to keep his feelings about the divorce in check. Darren had a feeling his mom wanted him to stay close, so she could keep an eye on him.

"Both of your parents will see this trip as a nice change of pace for you—a chance to get out of the house and spend time in nature," Mr. Kimura added.

"Do you think so?" Darren asked, his mood lifting. "I really want to go."

"And we want you there with us," Mack said. "I need some serious competition for my flame throwing, and I bet no other kid in the country is half as good as we are."

Darren laughed. "I'll definitely ask my mom," he said. "It would be cool to finally meet another *impundulu*."

"We have lots of work ahead of us," Ms. Therian said with a smile, "but not today. The First Four have plans for the Youngling Games to review."

"Can I look at *The Compendium* before my father gets here?" Fiona asked. "I'd love to find out what it has to say about Wyndemere Academy."

"Of course," Mr. Kimura answered. "Makoto can get it for you."

Darren, Fiona, and Gabriella plopped onto the floor in Mack's bedroom while he ran off to get *The Compendium*. The bookshelves in Mack's room were filled with comic books, and the walls were lined with comic-book art.

"I can't believe there's a whole school just for Changers," Fiona said. "I thought everyone was just trained by a family member or by someone from the Changer nation, in small groups, like we are."

"I can't believe the vision of us all," Gabriella interjected. "I mean, Mack had nine tails! And he didn't look that old, either. And Fiona, you were—"

"Doing something my mother said I would do one day," Fiona whispered, the realization donning on her. "I was bringing the selkies back to the Changer nation. . . . At least, that's what it looked like. Gabriella, you were a superhero, just like your aunt!"

Gabriella laughed. "I wonder if I really will be the Jade Jaguar someday, just like in the comic I made with Mack."

Fiona's eyes lit up. "And Darren—those people—it looked like you were making new Changers! Is that even possible?"

Darren shrugged. "I'm still trying to figure out why I'm a Changer at all," he said. "You three have family members who are Changers. I don't know anyone in my family who has the ability."

"Maybe you don't, but that doesn't mean you aren't related to another *impundulu*," Gabriella said. "I was totally shocked when I learned Tía Rosa and my *abuelita* were Changers. Maybe you have family members who haven't revealed themselves to you yet."

Darren was mentally running through his family tree, trying to figure out who might be a Changer. He almost laughed at the thought of his uncle Harvey, who already had a long beak-like nose, transforming into a bird.

Mack showed up with The Compendium and handed it to Fiona. She and Darren had found the ancient book earlier this year in the rare books room of New Brighton University's library. The Compendium had helped them learn about the Horn of Power and locate Circe's

Compass, but the book guarded its secrets. Whenever Darren picked up *The Compendium*, he'd rarely ever read the same passage twice—the book changed each time he opened it.

Fiona carefully turned the pages, looking for information about Wyndemere Academy or the Youngling Games.

"Ms. Therian said that Wyndemere was the only school for Changers in the country," she said. "Do you think there are other schools in other parts of the world?"

"Makes sense," Mack said.

Almost as soon as Fiona asked the question, the answer appeared on a page about Changer boarding schools.

"'Many countries have their own academies,'" she read. "Look at this one in Italy! How old do you think it is? Do you think they allow students to take a semester abroad like colleges do?"

Gabriella laughed. "Why don't we find out about the school in *this* country first?"

Fiona turned the page, and the words, which had

been jumbled and looked as if there were written in another language a second before, began to sort themselves out into English words.

"'The campus of Wyndemere Academy is situated in a remote forested area along the coast and housed in a castle that is more than two hundred and fifty years old,'" she read. "'A cloaking spell is performed each spring by Mr. Akira Kimura, First Four, Class A, nine-tailed *kitsune*, to hide it from the non-magical world.'"

Darren eyed Mack to see if he had had any clue about his grandfather's cloaking spells, but he looked as surprised as the rest them. "What else?" Mack asked.

"'The application period runs from September to March, and students are notified of acceptance in late spring. The student body has around fifteen hundred students, aged fourteen to eighteen.'"

Darren whistled. "I had no idea there were that many of us."

"And that's just in the United States," Mack added.

"'All Changer younglings are welcome to apply, and tuition is free to those whose parents have sworn fealty to the Changer nation.'" Fiona paused for a moment, and Darren wondered if she was thinking about her mother—the *selkie* queen. The *selkies* had split off from the Changer nation when Fiona was just three. Fiona was told that her mother had died, but in truth, Leana Murphy had left Fiona and her father so that she could lead the *selkies*. Fiona had reconnected with her mother just before the final battle with Auden Ironbound, and now she was learning the *selkie* songs from her.

Will Fiona's selkie *heritage prevent her from going to Wyndemere someday?* Darren wondered. He was sure it couldn't be true—Fiona was one of the next leaders of the Changers. . . . There was no chance they would turn her away, right?

Gabriella nudged Fiona gently, and Fiona continued reading. "'Classes are held from September to June; dormitories are on-site. The lagoon is open year-round to waterborne Changers. Special accommodations are made to ensure that the children of non-Changer parentage are able to attend.'"

Darren peered over Fiona's shoulder and watched as a sketch of the Wyndemere campus appeared. He and his family had toured some New England colleges when Ray was checking out schools, and Wyndemere's castle looked like some of the Gothic mansions they'd seen along the coast. It was very big and very old.

A much more modern sports stadium appeared on the next page, and younglings of various types were seen competing in magical events. "Wow! Look at that," Gabriella said. "This is going to be so cool."

"Hey! Doesn't that look like the same kind of bear Changer we saw in the vision of Circe's apprentices?" Mack asked, pointing to a bear that was squaring off against a jaguar. "I'm going to get so much inspiration for my *Kitsune Tails* comic."

"Oh, look at the lagoon," Fiona said.

Even Darren found himself getting excited about the trip, in spite of everything that was going on at home. He was still amazed and confused sometimes about his incredible new powers. Keeping them a secret at home was hard, and to finally be able to talk to another *impundulu*—to meet someone who understood these powers, to hear about how they got through such an enormous change—it would be, well, *freeing*.

He only hoped his mom would let him go.

Darren waved good-bye to Ms. Therian and Sefu after they dropped him off at his house that night. His mom was up in her room, likely working on a new paper for her lab.

Full of the courage that Mr. Kimura's words had given him, he climbed the stairs two at a time and lightly knocked on his mom's doorframe. Mom was already in her pj's, rubbing her temples as she stared into her laptop. The bed was strewn with research papers from various chemistry journals.

"You're home early," Mom said, sitting up a little straighter against the headboard. "I figured you'd be out with your friends past dinnertime."

"Ray and I are video-chatting tonight, so I wanted to make sure I was home a little early," Darren said.

His mom reached out her hand for his. "I'm so glad you two have each other to talk to, going through everything. It's comforting to your father and me."

Darren wasn't sure what to say. It was still a little painful anytime his mom brought up the divorce.

"Anyway," she cut back in. "Why don't we order

some takeout tonight? Maybe that Thai place on Market Street? I know you like their curry."

"Sure, Mom. Sounds good," Darren said, trying to find the right way to broach the subject of the field trip. "There's something I wanted to talk to you about."

Darren handed his mom the packet Ms. Therian had given him. His mom removed the papers from the envelope and started rifling through them.

"There's a class field trip coming up over spring break, and I really want to go."

"Isn't Ms. Therian your gym teacher?" Mom asked as she read the first page.

For a panicked moment Darren wasn't sure what to say. Then he remembered the third page of the packet.

"Here," Darren said, turning the pages. "It's actually a joint trip between gym, social studies, and science class. Identifying the geography and learning about the life cycle of plants is one part of the trip, but there're also a lot of hiking and outdoor activities too. That's why Ms. Therian is heading it. I think it would be a lot of fun—Gabriella, Mack, and Fiona said they're definitely going. . . ."

"You know what?" Mom said, flipping to the last page.

Darren was hanging on the edge of his seat, waiting for his mother's response.

"I think this is wonderful." She took out her pen and signed the permission slip, handing it and the rest of the papers back to him. "And what a great use of your spring break. I'd much rather have you outdoors learning something than sleeping past noon and playing video games like you usually do."

"Hey!" Darren shouted.

His mom punched him in the shoulder playfully and reached for her phone to order their dinner. Darren smiled as he stared at the permission slip in his hand. He was really going to Wyndemere! Who would he meet; what would he learn while he was there?

Darren had no clue, but if it was half as interesting as this morning's meeting had been, he couldn't wait.

Chapter 3
Wyndemere Academy

A few weeks later Fiona swam through an obstacle course in the gym's saltwater pool, her final training day for the Youngling Games. She'd said her good-byes to Dad a few hours ago, and her luggage, along with Gabriella's, was neatly stacked in the locker room. Ms. Therian said they had time for one last training session before they left, and she had hidden a tiny treasure in the pool, using enchantments to create obstacles and make the water dark and murky. But in her *selkie* form, Fiona's eyes caught every nuance in the water. Fiona could now stay under for about an hour without having to come up for air, but today, she needed less than half of that for her sharp eyes to find the gold ring in the pool's hazy depths. She grabbed the ring with her mouth and shot out of the water, triumphant.

Over the past few weeks she and her friends had trained hard for the Youngling Games. Gabriella had signed up for three separate events: the enchanted hurdles, the agility course, and timed combat. Mack and Darren were both competing in an elemental archery contest. They had spent the month learning how to transform their fire (in Mack's case) and lightning (in Darren's) into bows and arrows. Darren had also signed up for a competition that involved deflecting magic spells.

"Just let them try to get past my lightning force fields," Darren had joked. "They'd be toast!"

Fiona couldn't believe how brave he and Gabriella were to sign up for more than one event. Despite her training, Fiona was nervous about the underwater treasure hunt in Wyndemere Academy's lagoon. Not about whether or not she could finish the course; she knew she could do *that*. It was having to compete against other waterborne Changers and trying to best them in a physical competition. Fiona was worried that she'd come in last. Sports had never really been her thing. She'd be much more confident taking a written test or researching a paper. That was the kind of competition she knew she'd win.

She sat by the side of the pool and watched Darren fire a lightning arrow at a target, and then Ms. Therian blew her whistle to signal the end of their practice.

Fiona slipped off her *selkie* cloak and ran down to the locker room to wash off and change. Minutes later she grabbed her duffel bag and joined the others around their teacher. A beautiful Japanese woman with bright eyes had joined them.

"I want you to meet Margery Haruyama, a *tengu* Changer," Ms. Therian said.

"What's a *tengu*?" Mack asked.

"She's a bird Changer—like me," Darren said, beating Fiona to the answer. "She has power over wind."

"That's right," Margery said with a friendly smile. "I have another power, too—the power to transport you anywhere you want to go in the blink of an eye."

Mack whistled. "Anywhere?"

She nodded. "Anywhere."

Fiona could tell by the way his eyes lit up that he was thinking about all the cool places he'd like to go. But today they were going to Wyndemere Academy!

Ms. Therian reached for Fiona's hand. "Join hands," she said, "and we'll be off."

There was a *whoosh*, and for a moment, Fiona felt like she was nestled inside the calm heart of the wind. For two or three dizzying seconds the world flew by, and then they landed gently at the base of a grassy hill. On top of it was a familiar-looking Gothic castle.

Before they even had time to say thank you, Margery spun on her heel and was gone in a flash.

Fiona twirled around as she took in as much of the buildings and the grounds as she could see. The academy was even more incredible looking in person.

"This is where I leave you," Ms. Therian said. "I'm going to help with the preparation for the games. I'll be around in case you need me, but *only* if you need me. This weekend should be about exploring, trying new things, and meeting as many Changers as you can."

Fiona suddenly felt a little scared at the idea of Ms.

Therian leaving them on their own for a few days.

Ms. Therian seemed to read her thoughts. "You're safe here—the grounds are protected from intruders of all kinds, magic or otherwise. Akira's protection spells are in place, and there are Changer soldiers patrolling the forest."

Mack swaggered a few feet up the hill. Fiona could tell that he liked the idea of hanging out with high school kids without the First Four hovering over the four of them. "Don't worry about us," he said.

"I'm trusting you not to wander off into the forest," Ms. Therian said a bit louder, eyeing Mack in particular. "Stay on the school's grounds. And don't go looking for trouble."

"Will do," Mack said with a nod. "It's time to warn these high schoolers that a bunch of seventh graders are about to tear up the Youngling Games."

Ms. Therian laughed and waved them toward the top of the hill. "First you need to register for the games," she said, "or you won't be 'tearing up' anything."

The kids scrambled up the hillside, cheering as they raced to be the first to get to the top. After just one or two steps, Gabriella was far in front of the others, and she beat them to the school. She waited for them just outside of the reception area.

"Names, please," a woman sitting behind a desk said. After checking their names against her list, she gave each of them a tote bag and told them to report to their dormitories. "Someone will be waiting in the lobby to give you your room assignments."

"I can't believe we get to stay in dorm rooms," Fiona said. "I hope we get to be roommates." She linked her arm with Gabriella's, and they headed in the direction of the girls' dorm.

"Catch you later," Mack said, jogging off toward the boys' dorm with Darren.

Fiona was even more impressed by the campus now that she was here. It was kind of like being at New Brighton University. But on this campus the air shimmered with magic. High school–aged kids confidently walked to and from their classes, calling out hellos and asking one another if they were ready for this test or that science lab. However, there was something different.

Fiona watched a girl who was across the green transform into a werewolf, let out a giant howl, and then change back to her human self. The kids around her laughed, as if she was making a joke or had just proved a point.

Gabriella laughed along with them. "It's nice not having to worry about my eyes suddenly turning yellow or my claws popping out and scaring our classmates," she said.

Fiona nodded, gazing longingly at the books each student carried. They had titles like *Relics of Our Past: Enchanted Objects and Their Uses* and *A History of Temples, Tombs, and Other Mystical Sites.*

"I bet the library here is amazing—like one huge version of the rare books room at New Brighton University. Where do you think it is?"

Gabriella shrugged. "We'll find it later. There's the girls' dorm."

The dorm was at the far end of the castle grounds, an old building that looked like mansions she'd seen in books about New England. The inside matched the imposing exterior. There was a huge foyer and a grand staircase leading up to the second, third, and fourth floors. Paintings of mythological creatures lined the walls. *No, not mythological,* Fiona reminded herself. *Real. Changers.*

A pretty girl with a friendly smile stood in the foyer with a clipboard and introduced herself as Zahra, a junior at Wyndemere. "I'll be your guide and resident adviser for the week," she said. "I'm the person you come to with any questions," she added, after seeing Gabriella's blank stare. Zahra checked their names against her list. "You're both in room 206. Why don't you go up and unpack while I wait for a few more people to arrive?"

Fiona was excited to discover that room 206 was in one of the towers. Their circular room had four beds in it, and two other girls were unpacking. She and Gabriella introduced themselves.

"I'm Mindy—I'm a *mo'o* from Hawaii," the first girl said.

Fiona was glad that she had studied Changer forms so she didn't have to ask Mindy what a *mo'o* was—she was a Hawaiian water dragon.

The second, a beautiful girl with caramel-colored

skin and long, dark silky hair introduced herself as Jess. "I'm a mermaid—also from Hawaii," she said with a smile. Her eyes seemed to shift from green to blue to gray in the light.

Fiona was about to tell Jess and Mindy that she was a waterborne Changer too when Zahra whistled from the hall, telling the residents to bring their welcome bags and join her for orientation. Twenty girls gathered around Zahra. Most of them, Fiona noticed, were nervously peeking at the others, just as she was. She was glad to have Gabriella at her side.

Having friends her own age was a new experience for Fiona. Sure, she had always had kids in school to talk to, but she'd never had a best friend or been invited to hang out outside of school. The other girls were nice to her, mostly, but she sat alone on the bus and, until she befriended Gabriella, in the school cafeteria, too.

She had mostly told herself that it didn't matter, that her books were the only friends she really needed. She used the extra time on the bus and at lunch for homework and for reading. But now that Fiona had real friends like Gabriella, Mack, and Darren, she realized that she had always been a little sad without people her own age to talk to.

Fiona hoped that here, at Wyndemere Academy, she'd make even more friends.

Zahra clapped her hands for attention. "Besides the fifteen hundred Changers that attend Wyndemere, there are about one hundred and fifty kids here for the games, but this is your group of twenty," she said. "I want to show you what's in your welcome bags, and then we'll take a tour of the campus."

One by one she pulled items out of her own welcome bag and explained what they were, which included a map of the campus, a list of emergency contacts, a booklet about the school and its history, a schedule of Youngling Games events, and a class schedule.

Fiona's eyes lit up. A class schedule! She hadn't realized that they'd get to sit in on classes, too. She wanted to take a look at hers right away and wondered if there would be time to visit more than one class, but Zahra had already moved on.

"There are some snacks and bottled water in here too, and don't be shy about replenishing from the dining hall. It's open twenty-four seven, so take whatever you need. There are also snacks in the dorm's lounge down the hall. We want you at your best for the games, not tired and hungry."

Moments later, Zahra led them outside for a tour of the grounds. Fiona had read everything she could about the academy, but Zahra ran through the highlights.

"Wyndemere Academy—both the building and the campus—was built in 1743 from local limestone deposits as a refuge for Changer-kind in North America.

"The academy functioned as a Changer base for thirty years before Ilyana the Conqueror converted it into a school for younglings, aged fourteen to eighteen," Zahra continued. "By that time, other Changer bases around the country had been established."

Fiona knew that the town of Willow Cove had an important Changer base and that a Changer base was more commonly called a "harbor." For the first time she wondered how many Changer bases there were in the world. She was about to raise her hand to ask, but once again, Zahra had already moved on. It sounded to Fiona as if she had given this speech many times.

"There are eight main buildings on campus," she said. "The girls' dorm and the boys' dorm are on opposite ends of the campus. The boys' dorm is off limits to girls, and vice versa." Then she pointed to what looked like a sports stadium. "There's the arena and the games house, where the events will take place. And next to that is the gymnasium. If you have any last-minute training to do, that's the place to go. And of course," she said, waving toward the four connected buildings that made up the castle, "those are the four academic buildings."

They walked to the arena first, which was a whirlwind of preparation activity. An *impundulu* and a *tengu*, both in bird form, were hanging a welcome banner. Fiona's heart soared at the sight of the lightning bird. *Looks like Darren will definitely have other impundulus to talk to!* Ms. Therian and some other adult Changers were overseeing the setup of an enchanted hurdles course. Ms. Therian snapped her fingers, and the hurdles moved, up and down, up and down. Then one burst into flames.

Gabriella was rocking back and forth on her heels, clearly itching to take on the hurdles, but Zahra hurried them out of the stadium and into the gym next door. Fiona gasped when she saw the many, many different forms of Changers doing last-minute training exercises. She noticed there was no saltwater pool like the one in Willow Cove's enchanted gym, but then she remembered that the lagoon was open all year long. That's where her event would take place.

If only I didn't have to actually compete, she thought, feeling butterflies in her stomach. *I hope I don't embarrass myself . . . or my friends.*

She asked a question about history to get her mind off the competition. "Are the Youngling Games like the Olympics? Do they take place every four years?"

"The games were started in the early 1900s as a way to introduce young Changers to Wyndemere Academy before the application period ended for incoming freshmen. It's a yearly event."

"And anyone—any young Changer can compete?"

"Oh, no," Zahra said. "Wyndemere students have their own athletic competitions throughout the year. Only Changers between the ages of eleven and thirteen are able to compete in the Youngling Games. This year we have competitors from all over the country, even Hawaii."

Fiona sneaked a quick peek at Jess and Mindy. They seemed pleased to have been singled out.

Zahra waved in the direction of the door. "You can come back to explore the arena and the gym later. First I want to give you a quick tour of the academic buildings."

The small group entered the castle, filing past a group of twenty boys, including Mack and Darren, that was on its way out.

"Wait till you see the art studio," Mack whispered.

"Wait till you see the gym," Gabriella whispered back.

The main entry hall of the academic buildings, like the girls' dorm, was massive and ornate, with mahogany paneling and a grand staircase. Marble carvings along the walls showed Changers locked in epic battles, exploring new places, and building huge structures. Fiona took a deep breath. She could almost smell the rich history and important learning that went on here.

Zahra waited a moment to make sure she had

everyone's attention before speaking. "The second, third, and fourth floors are mainly classrooms and professors' offices," she said. "We're just going to tour the first floor." Then she quickly led them from one amazing room to another—an auditorium, a band room filled with music stands and instruments and soundproof practice rooms, a student lounge for games and hanging out, and a dining hall that offered all kinds of delicious food.

Fiona wanted to stop and investigate everything, but Zahra hurried them along, promising that they would have time to come back and explore later.

The art studio was next. It was huge, with great big windows overlooking the campus, and every kind of art supply you could imagine, including easels and drawing tables. Gabriella spotted someone working on a comic book. "I can see why Mack was so excited about the art studio," she said.

"I can't wait to see the library," Fiona whispered back. "I bet it's amazing."

A minute later Fiona got her wish. A shiver of excitement ran up her spine as they stepped into the library. It had the same delicious smell as any library, but this one had something extra. Something magical.

The library was the full height of the castle—no classrooms or offices were above this room. Tall bookshelves lined the walls from floor to ceiling. Three balconies wrapped around the walls of the room so students could access the books. It was the most amazing library Fiona could imagine.

Before she could take it all in, Zahra swept them back outside. Fiona blinked in the sunshine, her mind still in the library. There had been stained-glass windows that seemed to tell a story, but Fiona hadn't had time to "read" them and figure it out.

"I'm definitely coming back here," she said to Gabriella.

"That's the end of our tour," Zahra said when they were back outside. "There's just one more thing." Again, she stopped to make sure that everyone in the group was listening before she spoke, and then she pulled out her campus map and pointed to a tower in the northeast corner of the castle.

"There's construction going on in the northeast tower, so please avoid that area of the castle," she said, her voice suddenly very stern. "It's not safe, so don't go poking around there, got it?"

Zahra's manner lightened up. "And now you're free to explore or have dinner or train for your events. Get to know one another. You may all be coming to high school here in a year or two."

"Dinner?" Fiona asked Gabriella.

She nodded. "I'm starving, and that food smelled really good."

Fiona asked Mindy and Jess to join them, and the four girls found their way back to the dining hall. Mack and Darren were across the room, deep in conversation with some other boys.

The girls grabbed some food—veggie pasta for Fiona, Jess, and Mindy, and steak for Gabriella—and found seats at a table. They compared notes about their competitions. Not surprisingly, both Jess and Mindy were participating in the same underwater treasure hunt as Fiona. They had both signed up for an underwater race, too.

"I have to warn you—I'm going to dominate," Mindy said with a smile.

"That's fine with me," Fiona said. "Sports aren't exactly my favorite thing. Gabriella, on the other hand, is going to win all of her events—she's totally amazing."

"Fiona's going to do great," Gabriella said, elbowing her friend. "I have no doubt that she's the fastest *selkie* here."

Jess's smile disappeared, and she dropped her fork. "You're a *selkie*?"

Fiona nodded.

"But—what are you doing here," Mindy asked. There was a hard edge to her voice.

It didn't really sound like a question. It sounded like a challenge. It was almost as if Mindy was ready to fight.

Fiona felt her cheeks burning. Why had Mindy and Jess suddenly gotten so angry? She struggled to find an answer to Mindy's question.

Gabriella had no such trouble. "Why shouldn't she be here?" she asked, angry on her friend's behalf. "She's a Changer, just like you."

Mindy's cheeks turned red. "It's just that most *selkies* belong to the *selkie* faction. They split from the Changers a long time ago. They don't want anything to do with us."

"There are rumors that the *selkies* are traitors to the Changer nation, that they've teamed up with dark witches and warlocks," Jess said with a concerned expression. "How do we know you're not a spy?"

The word "traitors" made Fiona cringe. She knew that the *selkies* weren't traitors (just stubborn and proud), but she couldn't reveal how she knew that without raising more suspicion. She shook her head. "Of course I'm not a spy," she said.

She wanted to tell them more, but the First Four had warned her not to tell anyone else about her mom being the *selkie* queen. She hadn't realized that Changer distrust of the *selkies* ran so deep. She knew her mother would never betray the Changers—*never*. How could she defend herself against Jess's and Mindy's accusations without telling the truth?

Once again, Gabriella jumped to her friend's defense, her eyes flashing. "The Changers took Fiona in, and we're really lucky they did. She has some awesome powers."

"What kind of Changer are you?" Jess asked Gabriella nervously.

"I'm a *nahual*," Gabriella answered. "A black jaguar *nahual*," she added, still a bit angry.

Mindy gasped. Jess's eyes widened.

"Are you two from Willow Cove?" Jess and Mindy asked, both at the same time.

Gabriella and Fiona looked at each other, their eyebrows raised. Before they could answer, Mindy rushed to explain—and apologize.

"You're the ones who took down Auden Ironbound!" she said to Fiona. "I'm so sorry—I didn't mean to be rude earlier. We heard all about you. Everybody did. You guys are heroes."

"We didn't mean anything by what we said. We've just never met a *selkie* before," Jess added. "We've always been warned to stay away from the ones in the waters around Hawaii. They're just sort of . . . scary-protective of their territory."

Fiona would have laughed at the idea of people finding her scary, but this whole conversation made her superuncomfortable. She was relieved when both Jess and Mindy awkwardly struggled to change the subject, but at the same time her mind whirled with questions.

What if I really don't belong here? If the Changers believe my mom is a traitor and that selkies are spies, I won't ever fit in. Will Wyndemere Academy accept my friends and reject me because I'm my mother's daughter?

Chapter 4
FOLLOWED

Early the next morning Mack woke up to a text message from Joel Hastings, his best friend. Mack and Joel had drifted apart a bit ever since Mack found out he was a Changer, but Joel was still his closest friend.

How's the national park field trip going?

Mack rubbed the sleep from his eyes as he texted back.

Really fun. How's Spain?

Awesome! I picked up some comic books in Spanish for you—they're really cool.

Bring me a pinecone?

Mack snorted.

Ha. Ha. We can't all go on amazing, globe-trotting spring break vacations, Joel.

So that's a no on the pinecone?

Mack smiled as he set his phone to the side and got out of bed. Joel had texted pretty early due to the time difference, but Mack didn't mind—he was excited for his first full day at Wyndemere. It was neat getting to see the campus yesterday, but today Mack really wanted to talk to some of the other students and find out more about their Changer forms and magical abilities. If there was time he'd head to the art studio to work on sketches for his *Kitsune Tails* comic.

Mack's comic book for the end-of-the-year middle-school art show was going to be killer. The kids at Willow Cove Middle School would believe he was making up stories about mythological shape-shifters, but Mack was drawing inspiration from real life. . . . And he was about to get some insider info.

Darren was as excited to start his day as Mack was. They had just sat down with loaded breakfast trays— the Wyndemere dining hall was the best—when Fiona and Gabriella joined them.

"Let's compare schedules," Mack said, pulling a piece of paper from his welcome bag.

The others did the same, and Mack scanned them for similarities.

"We both have Defense Tactics for Land-Based Changers after breakfast," Mack said to Gabriella. "Cool."

Fiona read the name of her class out loud. "'Changer Perceptions After the Turn of the First Millennium, CE,'" she said.

Mack wrinkled his nose. "History?"

Fiona laughed. "I love history. And that's my only class. I was going to try to sit in on a few more, but then I got a look at the library. I think I'll spend the rest of the day exploring that. What about you, Darren?"

"My class is Changer Mythology: Separating Fact from Fiction," he said, reading his schedule. "And I noticed there's a movie club meeting this afternoon. I think I'll check it out. It's the most normal thing about this place."

Gabriella gave him a playful punch on the arm. "This is *all* normal," she said with a laugh. "It's normal for Changers, and we *are* Changers."

"Okay, okay," Darren said, raising his hands in surrender. "I'm just taking a little bit longer than the rest of you to get used to this whole secret magical world thing. There are still some mornings when I wake up and think I dreamed it all. But since I got a handle on my powers, it doesn't feel like a nightmare anymore—just a really strange dream."

"At least you're going to do great at your event in the games," Fiona commented.

"I hope so," Darren said.

"You're going to kick butt, Darren. . . . Except for the event we're competing in together," Mack joked. "I'm planning to win that one." Then he turned to Gabriella. "Ready to go?"

Gabriella took one last bite of her eggs, and they headed to class.

A tall blond woman waited for them in the center of the grassy quad. "Welcome. I'm Professor Leifsson," she said. "I'm a *nykur*, or horse Changer from Iceland. We'll be practicing defensive moves out here today while the gym is being prepped for the games."

She Changed and then thought to the group, *Who*

wants to show me some defensive moves while I attack? Don't worry. I won't hurt anyone.

Mack felt a surge of confidence. He spent almost every afternoon training with Gabriella, and he'd fought alongside the First Four. It was time to show Wyndemere what he was made of. Without a second thought, he Changed and stepped forward. *Bring it on,* he thought. *And don't go easy on me.* He could see some of the others in the class eyeing his two tails. It was unusual for a young *kitsune* to have already earned a second tail.

He wondered for a moment if Professor Leifsson would have anything to teach him; he didn't expect *nykurs* to have the kind of agility a *kitsune* or a *nahual* did, but his professor was amazingly fast. Mack quickly regretted his cocky behavior when his teacher went into attack mode. He tried to defend himself, but she bested him once, twice, and then three times. Total humiliation!

Now, would anyone like to tell me why the kitsune's *defensive tactics didn't work against me?* she asked.

Mack cringed, but luckily, no one in the big group could answer her question.

So instead, Professor Leifsson showed them some powerful moves that would have worked against her attacks, and Mack couldn't help but be impressed. At the end of two hours, he was exhausted. He also had a lot more tools and maneuvers at his disposal, in case he was ever attacked.

"If any warlock comes after us again, we'll make mincemeat out of him," Mack said to Gabriella after they transformed back into their human forms.

"I hope it never comes to that," Gabriella said with a frown. "I'm going to check out the arena again. Maybe some of the coaches are around. Want to come?"

Mack shook his head. "I'm going to work on ideas for my comic," he said. He watched her go, and then he grabbed a seat on a bench, making quick sketches of his *nykur* professor, and a bear Changer in their class— whom he learned was called an *ijiraat*—from memory. Then he started checking out the students around him. He had planned to interview them about their abilities and powers, but after getting beaten so badly in front of everyone in class, he felt a little awkward.

Even so, he kept his eyes open, and every once in

a while he saw a transformation he hadn't seen before. He tried not to think and just keep his hand moving as he watched a *mujina*, a Japanese badger Changer, demonstrate something to a *púca*, an Irish ram Changer.

Minutes later, a giant serpent, whom Mack recognized as a *naga*, slithered through the grass in front of him, came up behind a girl, and tapped her on the shoulder!

Mack kept sketching, letting his mind wander. It wasn't long before he was thinking about the golden *kitsune* he saw on the battlefield nearly four months ago.

Why won't Jiichan talk about her? The First Four were more than a little freaked out when I told them I saw her at the battle on the beach. What could she have done that was so bad?

In all of Fiona's research in The *Compendium*, she had never once encountered word of an evil *kitsune*. So what was the big secret?

Suddenly, Mack felt eyes on him. He turned to look, and there she was—the golden *kitsune*—staring at him from the tree line. Mack felt almost hypnotized while she held his gaze. Then she cocked her head, turned, and disappeared into the forest.

For a moment, Mack remembered Jiichan's serious tone, the worry in his eyes, when the golden *kitsune* was mentioned. *Could this be a trap?* Mack wondered. The streak of fur was getting farther away in the distance. If Mack truly wanted answers, it was now or never. With one last look at his notebook, Mack got up and ran in her direction, heading into the trees, not thinking at all about Ms. Therian's warnings to stay out of the forest.

Deeper and deeper into the woods he ran, catching only a glimpse of her at every turn until all he saw was a gold streak in the distance.

Mack grimaced. It was like she was taunting him to follow her. Why wouldn't she wait for him?

Then suddenly, she stopped. *I have a message for you,* she said. Her voice was soothing, but there was a sense of urgency to her words.

Mack stumbled a few steps forward, but a shadow passed over him, and he looked up at the sky. Was it about to get dark? When Mack turned back to her, the golden *kitsune* had gone. He ran forward, jumping over a fallen tree—had he done something wrong? She had something to tell him; why would she leave? He was about to transform so he could run faster when a deep voice stopped him.

"Hey, kid!" A Wyndemere guard ran over and stood in front of him. "What are you doing in the woods?"

"Sorry," Mack said, scrambling for an excuse. "Just walking. I—I thought I saw something."

"There's nothing out here except trees." The guard pointed in the direction of the campus. "Back to the lawn," he said. "It's dangerous for younglings to wander around alone in the forest."

Mack was about to point out to the guard that if there was really nothing out there but trees, then it wouldn't be dangerous to wander around alone, but the look on the guard's face stopped him.

Mack turned and trudged back to the center of campus feeling angry and frustrated. The golden *kitsune* was trying to tell him something. Something Jiichan didn't want him to know.

I need to find her, and hear what she has to say. Even if it's something the First Four don't think I'm ready to hear.

Chapter 5
WYNDEMERE'S FASTEST

While Mack was sketching, Gabriella headed down to the sports arena to watch the preparation for the games. She wanted to scope out the enchanted hurdles and the agility courses before the big day. Even though she was confident she could win both of her events, it always helped knowing what to expect.

There was almost nothing she loved more than a competition, in or out of her *nahual* form. *This is going to be so cool!* she thought.

The arena was full of groups of high schoolers setting up and testing equipment for the games. Gabriella took a seat halfway up the bleachers, where she could see everything. Then she reluctantly pulled out the homework her math teacher had assigned for spring break. Homework over break was totally unfair, but she knew that the sooner she got it done, the sooner she could forget about it and concentrate on the competition. She had one eye on her homework and the other on the kids setting up equipment for the various contests.

Most of the kids were on the other side of the arena, working on what looked like a giant game of mousetrap. One guy was closer to Gabriella, setting up an equally massive obstacle course by himself. She thought she saw the scaffolding he was building sway. *Some kind of magic,* she thought.

Then the scaffolding wobbled.

The guy was standing next to it, reading blueprints. He wore headphones and bobbed his head to the music.

And then the scaffolding actually shook.

It didn't look like magic anymore. It looked like the scaffolding was about to collapse, right on top of the guy—and he had no idea what was coming.

"Watch out!" Gabriella shouted.

But, of course, he couldn't hear her warning over his music.

In a flash, without thinking, Gabriella transformed and bounded across the field. She pushed the guy out of the way and leaped to safety just as the scaffolding came crashing down, right where he had been standing a second before.

Barely winded, Gabriella transformed back into her human form.

The guy stared at her and then at the heap of boards and metal at his feet. "Wow, I think you saved my life," he said. "Thank you."

Other student volunteers ran over and started whistling and applauding. For a second, Gabriella thought back to the vision of herself as a superhero that they'd seen in the moonstone.

Maybe saving people really is what I'm meant to do.

Gabriella was both proud and a little embarrassed. "I saw you needed help, and I was the closest," she said with a shrug.

"We're shorthanded," he said. "I should have had

someone holding the frame up for me, but we've got too much to do before tomorrow and not enough people to do the work."

"Hey, would you want to help?" one of the girls asked Gabriella. "We could really use an extra set of hands."

Her homework forgotten, Gabriella readily agreed.

"Great, you're with Tony." Satisfied, the girl transformed into a bird, flew to the top of the arena, and adjusted the scoreboard.

Gabriella spent the rest of the day helping Tony, the guy she had saved. She thought she'd feel young and out of place at Wyndemere surrounded by all the high school kids, but she felt right at home. She and Tony made a good team.

Before long she was joking and laughing with him and the others while they set up equipment for various events, including two of her own.

"Hey, Gabriella, can you try out the agility course for us, make sure everything's good?" Tony asked.

"Are you kidding?" Gabriella asked. "I'd love—" She cut herself off. "Wait, is that against the rules? I don't want to disqualify myself."

Professor Leifsson was in the arena checking things out, so Tony called her over to ask.

"Is it against the rules for Gabriella to test the agility course for us?" he asked.

"I think it's fine," the *nykur* answered. "Once the course is up, anyone can come and try it out. I'm sure some of your competitors will be stopping by to run through it before the games."

The idea of her challengers running through the course lit Gabriella's competitive fire.

"Can someone time me?" she asked.

Tony pulled out his phone. "Ready?" he asked her.

Gabriella transformed, turned her yellow cat eyes on him, and nodded.

"Set," he said.

Gabriella crouched and blocked out everything except his voice and the finish line.

"Go!"

He hadn't even finished the word before Gabriella leaped down the track to the first obstacle. In an instant she took to the air, arching her back to slide through a hoop that burst into flames as she neared. Next, she dropped to the ground to weave in and out of a set of poles. An image of a flaming phoenix popped up as she made her way past the fifth pole, but Gabriella didn't flinch. There were enchanted tunnels and ladders and even a hurdle that raised and lowered itself when she came close, but Gabriella handled it all easily. She came to the end and jumped onto a platform, sorry that the game was over already.

It was only then that she heard the whistles and cheers.

"Fifty-two seconds!" Tony shouted, waving his phone. "That's a school record!"

Gabriella transformed back into her human self.

"We need you on the track team," someone yelled.

"How soon can you come to school here?" someone else asked.

Gabriella laughed. "I have to finish seventh grade first," she said. "Not to mention eighth."

As soon as they were finished packing up their tools and equipment, Tony and some of the others led her into the gym for some water. The bird-girl, whose name was Toula, joined them.

"I am seriously impressed," Gabriella said, looking around. The first time she'd been through the gym while on the tour, she hadn't had much time to look around. Now she saw that the sports facility was easily ten times the size of their enchanted gym at Willow Cove Middle School. She could do some intense training here, and have some even more intense fun.

"So what kind of sports teams do you have?" she asked.

"Track and field," Toula answered, "but it's nothing like the track and field you have at home. It's more like the agility course you just tore up. And the enchanted hurdles. There are all kinds of Changer sports that non-Changers could never even hope to participate in."

"We play some non-magical boarding schools in traditional sports, too, like soccer," Tony added. "They have no idea we're Changers. They just think we're awesome," he said with a laugh.

"Seriously, though, I hope you'll think about coming to Wyndemere for high school," Toula said.

Gabriella smiled. "I'll definitely think about it."

As they wandered through the rest of the facility,

Gabriella realized how much she *did* want to go to Wyndemere. She'd miss her soccer team, and especially her family and her normal friends. But she wouldn't be surprised if her Changer friends came to Wyndemere with her. And, of course, she had already made new friends here.

That's if her mother would agree to let her leave home for high school. Gabriella's *tía* Rosa was a *nahual* like her niece, but her mother had no idea about their magical world. She valued education, and she loved Gabriella and her younger sister Maritza more than anything. Gabriella wasn't sure her mother would be willing to let her leave home for four years before college.

Darren, too, had parents who had no idea about his magical abilities. He'd face the same kind of family obstacles that Gabriella would. She was still pondering those facts when she realized it was time for dinner, and she had promised to meet Fiona.

Before she left, Tony asked what contests she would be competing in.

"The agility course, enchanted hurdles, and timed combat," she answered.

"You're gonna do great," Toula said, raising her hand for a fist bump.

Gabriella met Toula's fist with her own, which felt oddly normal after the day's supernatural events.

"We'll be cheering you on," Tony said.

"Thanks," Gabriella said. "I can't wait till tomorrow!"

Chapter 6
BLOODLINES

After his Changer mythology class, Darren spent the day checking out the campus and practicing for his event. He could feel himself getting stronger, and he definitely had more control. When his Changer abilities first started to manifest, his powers often got away from him—especially when he was upset about something. Learning that he was a magical shape-shifter who could shoot lighting from his hands was more than a little confusing.

In the beginning Darren had a lot of power and few ways to channel it. The night he had learned that his parents were getting a divorce, his fear had caused a massive storm around his house. Luckily, Darren had never seriously hurt anyone with his lightning abilities, but from that point on, Darren made controlling his powers his main focus. He knew that his raw power was perhaps the strongest of his friends, and that made managing it all the more difficult.

Things had definitely gotten better since then. Ms. Therian had taught Darren a lot about keeping his powers in check. He worked on it every single day. Talking to his Changer friends and his big brother, Ray, about the divorce helped. Ray had no idea Darren was a Changer, but like Darren, he knew what it was like to be different. There weren't many other African American kids in Willow Cove, so Ray could definitely relate.

Between Ms. Therian, his Changer friends, and Ray, Darren began to feel less out of control and more confident. He even started to enjoy the idea of being a Changer. . . . That is, when he *wasn't* battling evil warlocks and feeling scared out of his mind.

Darren checked his phone to see what time it was. There was another class he wanted to sit in on, and he had lost track of the afternoon. He had to transform in order to make it to the academic buildings on time.

If anyone would have told me back in September that I'd actually like being an impundulu, he thought, *I would have said they were crazy. But now here I am, flying across a campus full of shape-shifters like it's nothing.*

He landed in front of the main entrance for the academic buildings, transformed, and took the stairs two at a time for Professor Zwane's class on West and South African mythologies.

Darren had learned about Professor Zwane's course that morning during his Changer mythology class. The teacher could see how interested Darren was, and suggested he sit in on Professor Zwane's advanced lecture for seniors that afternoon. Not only was the professor an *impundulu* like Darren, he was an expert on South African tribal mythology—the area of the world where *impundulus* originated.

Seconds before class was to begin, Darren slipped into a seat in the last row. He had always been interested in mythology. At Willow Cove Middle School he had learned about a lot of cool Greek, Egyptian, and even Chinese lore, but his teachers had never talked about

African myths. He didn't even know there were any.

Darren shook his head. He could almost hear Fiona's voice scolding him. *Not myths. Real!* She was right, and that made everything about the stories even cooler.

Professor Zwane started to talk about the *anansesem*, or "spider tales," in West African mythology. While the rest of the class took notes, Darren sat back and just listened, fascinated.

"Anansi—the trickster god of wisdom, culture, and storytelling—is perhaps the main reason why spider, or so-called *Anansi* Changers, have managed to emerge with their good reputation intact from the pages of non-Changer mythology," the teacher said. "In fact, one of the original First Four was a spider Changer who led the war against Morwyn, Circe's dark apprentice, which you should all remember from last year's readings." He went on to explain that spider Changers had a variety of superhuman abilities, including immense strength and speed. Also true to their namesake, *Anansi* Changers were primarily responsible for keeping Changer knowledge alive during the Time of the Dark.

There's that phrase again, Darren thought. He and

Fiona first came across the term a few months ago, when they were doing research in *The Compendium* on Circe's Compass, but they had never figured out what it meant. He made a mental note to ask Fiona if they could find a book about the mysterious Time of the Dark in the library later.

"Without that wisdom, Changer history might have been lost in the battle against Morwyn and her followers over the millennia," Professor Zwane said.

Darren was spellbound. The First Four had never told them any stories from history like these.

Before he was even aware that he was doing it, Darren raised his hand.

"I see we have a youngling visitor who is brave enough to ask a question," Professor Zwane said with a smile. The rest of the students in the class craned their heads back to look at him. "Asking questions is how we learn, you know. You should all be doing more of that," the professor drawled out sarcastically. Then he turned to Darren. "Ask away, young man."

"I've, um, heard that Changer abilities can be passed down from generation to generation through bloodlines," he said. "But I've never heard of spider Changers before. Are they rare?"

"An excellent question," the professor answered. "Spider Changers have exceptionally powerful gifts, and the ability has been passed on, although only rarely. A small number of spider, or *Anansi* Changers, do exist today, primarily in Ghana."

While the professor went on to share some of the spider tales in West African folklore, Darren couldn't help but wonder about his own bloodline.

Are impundulus rare too? I feel like I've already seen two or three since coming here, not to mention Professor Zwane. So if they're not rare, then why am I the only one in my family with Changer abilities? And if I'm not the only one, why hasn't anyone come forward to tell me?

Darren was still thinking about this when he realized the other students were filing out of class. Professor Zwane was at the door and spoke to each student as he or she left, offering words of encouragement, reminding one guy that his research paper was late, and urging all of them to do the reading for next week's test.

Darren didn't expect a personal message, so he was

surprised when the professor signaled him to wait a moment.

"Do you have a minute to meet with me?" the professor asked. "My office is just down the hall."

Darren nodded, suddenly worried that maybe he shouldn't have asked a question after all, or that the professor had noticed he hadn't been paying attention at the very end of class. He followed Professor Zwane into his office, ready to be reprimanded.

An apology was already on Darren's lips, but instead of scolding him, the professor asked an unexpected question.

"Have you ever heard of the Spider's Curse?" he asked.

Darren shook his head. "The Spider's Curse? No. What's that?"

"The Spider's Curse is a powerful poison that comes from the bite of an *Anansi* Changer. They have the power to curse more than the individual they've bitten. The curse can course through the whole bloodline—passed down from generation to generation. This is especially true for *impundulu* bloodlines."

"*Impundulus?*" Darren asked. "But why us?"

Professor Zwane pulled a pen out of his desk and started scribbling on a piece of scrap paper. "In ancient times, before the Changer nation was established to prevent such things, there were sometimes wars between different Changer factions. Usually they had to do with establishing power over a particular area. There was a bitter conflict between the *Anansis* and the *impundulus* for many years."

Professor Zwane explained, "There was no clear winner before a truce was finally reached, but many of the *impundulus* were cursed. The Spider's Curse suppresses the Changer ability in a bloodline so that those under the curse can never use their Changer gifts. After the war, feelings were high on both sides, even with the truce. Most *Anansi* Changers refused to lift the curse, so it continues today."

Darren was stunned. "*Never* use their Changer gifts?" he repeated.

Professor Zwane nodded. "I could scarcely believe it—until I found out that I'm an *impundulu* who came from such a bloodline. When I was just a youngling, another *impundulu* recognized my ability, and also the curse," the professor said. "From the minute you walked into my classroom, I could sense that your power too is bound by it."

Chapter 7
The Spider's Curse

Your power too is bound by it.

The words hung in the air while questions raced through Darren's mind. How could his whole family be cursed? Were they in any danger? He was too stunned to even formulate full sentences.

"But . . . I definitely have my powers," Darren blurted. "In fact, sometimes I think I have *too much* power. There's no way I could be cursed."

Professor Zwane shook his head. "I'm afraid that I'm quite certain you are. I've experienced the weight of the curse before—I can feel its same hold on you."

The professor paused as he handed a piece of paper

to Darren. It read *The Anansi–Impundulu Wars by Dina Salawu.* Then he turned back to Darren. "This book should help. See if you can get it from the library before your stay here is over. Your power, it's . . . quite ancient. Can you summon lightning from within yourself, or do you need to channel it from the sky?"

"I can create it," Darren said, sounding a little frantic. "Is that bad?" He took a deep breath to get his racing heart under control.

The professor put a calming hand on Darren's arm. "It's not bad. That power is rare. It comes only from the most ancient and powerful *impundulu* bloodlines. Many of those bloodlines led the charge against the *Anansi,* and many of those bloodlines were cursed."

"Wait, that doesn't make any sense," Darren said. "You said the *impundulu* bloodlines were cursed to not be able to use the Changer gift, but I have it. So how did I become a Changer?"

"The same mysterious way I did," Professor Zwane answered. "All curses have laws. And all laws have loopholes. Somehow, you and I slipped through and came into our power despite the curse."

"So then . . . is it possible that there are other people in my family who are Changers, but the curse is blocking them from developing their powers as well?" Darren asked.

"It's certainly possible," the professor said with a nod.

"And if I break the curse, will they become Changers, or is it too late if they're older than twelve?"

"It's not too late," Professor Zwane said. "Most Changers start to develop powers in their twelfth year, but if a curse is broken, there's no age limit on transforming."

Darren thought about what a relief it would be to have another *impundulu* in the family—especially if that *impundulu* was Ray. For once, Darren would be the one to give help and advice to his big brother, instead of the other way around. That would be so cool. And it would be great to be able to be completely honest with Ray. Darren wasn't used to keeping secrets from his brother, and he definitely hated it.

But then again, Darren thought. *All those times I've wished these powers away . . . All the times I almost lost control, or was afraid I would hurt someone . . . Ray would have to deal with all of that too.* Suddenly, Darren wasn't so sure that breaking the curse was the best idea.

"If I wanted to . . . how could I break the curse?" Darren asked. "Can it be done?"

"It can be done, but it's not easy," Professor Zwane answered. "You'll have to find the *Anansi* Changer who cursed your bloodline—or one of his or her descendants—and get that person to grant their forgiveness."

"We're not at war anymore, right?" Darren asked. "So that shouldn't be too hard."

Professor Zwane seemed uncertain. "Some grudges last a long, long time—too long," he said. "There's also a chance that the particular *Anansi* Changer who cursed your bloodline has no descendants. Not all Changers bore Changer younglings. If your spider Changer died without having any children, then your family could suffer the curse forever."

"So if I can't find this spider's descendant, if their bloodline died out, I'm out of luck?" Darren slumped against the wall. "Has anyone ever gotten rid of the curse another way?" he asked. "Did you?"

"About a hundred years ago, there was a push to restore the lost *impundulu* bloodlines. Both the *Anansis* and the First Four worked some powerful magic. But that caused a lot of problems. Too many people started shifting into their *impundulu* forms and had powers that they hadn't yet learned to control. I'm sure you recognize how powerful our gift is. The lightning storms that ensued all over the planet were too fierce and too dangerous, especially for non-magical beings. But still, I was lucky enough to have my bloodline restored during this time. Now the First Four have special rules and safeguards in place for the curses. It can make the curse even harder to break."

"So what do I do now?" Darren asked. "Is it really hopeless?"

"This isn't cause for despair," Professor Zwane said. "You're particularly gifted. I can feel it. When you come of age you might yet find a way to break the curse, as I once did."

That made Darren feel a little better, but he still had questions. Questions he couldn't ask the professor without revealing the secret of the prophecy.

How could a cursed Changer become one of the new First Four? Maybe the prophecy is wrong and I'm not really destined to be a leader. Do Mr. Kimura and the others know about my curse? If they don't, what will they do when they find out? Maybe Circe will find someone to replace me.

Professor Zwane handed Darren his business card. "If you want to talk more about this or anything else, please don't worry about bothering me—get in touch any time."

"Thanks," Darren said, slipping it into his pocket. He probably would have a lot more questions, but right now, he needed to process what he had learned so far. It was all pretty confusing.

Darren trudged toward the dining hall. He was going to meet Mack for dinner, but all he could think about was the curse. He became increasingly angry with every step he took. *This is so not fair,* he thought. *Mack, Gabriella, and even Fiona have relatives who are Changers. They have someone to talk to about their abilities. They have help while I'm out here on my own.*

He thought about how much easier things would have been if Ray had been an *impundulu* too. He could've warned Darren about all the changes that were coming and walked him through them.

Stupid curse! Stupid, stupid curse!

Darren wasn't watching where he was going and banged right into Mack, who was hanging out in front of the dining hall.

"Hey—" Mack cut himself off when he got a look at Darren's face. "Everything all right, dude?"

Darren shook his head. "I just found out something I'm . . . not sure I wanted to know," he answered.

"Something you want to talk about?"

Darren brought Mack up to speed on the Spider's Curse and how he had somehow slipped through one of the curse's loopholes to become an *impundulu.*

"A curse that lasts for generations? That's seriously messed up," Mack said. "But at least now you know about it instead of being left in the dark. Lately I've been feeling like not knowing is a curse in and of itself."

"I guess," Darren said with a shrug. "But there's a lot more I don't know—like if I'll actually be able to break the curse and whether anyone else in my family is a Changer."

Mack frowned. "See? I hate not knowing things. I've been trying to get my grandfather to open up about that mysterious *kitsune* for months. Every time I ask a question about her, he shuts me down and tells me I'm not ready to hear what he has to say—like I'm a baby. Can you believe it?"

Darren shook his head. "Knowing. Not knowing. I'm not sure it makes a difference either way. Not when we can't *do* anything."

Darren peered into the dining room and wrinkled his nose. Suddenly, he wasn't hungry anymore, and Mack didn't look like he was ready for dinner either.

"Want to blow off some steam before we eat?" he asked. "I bet the sports arena is empty right now. We can practice our elemental archery ahead of the games tomorrow."

"Good idea," Mack said. "Let's go."

Chapter 8
The Memory Eater

Mack and Darren stood on one side of the sports arena, taking turns shooting flame and electric arrows at the practice targets on the other side. Mack was right about the place being empty. There was just one other Changer working out, a *naga*, or snake Changer, who was shooting water arrows at flaming targets across the range in her human form.

Ms. Therian had taught them how to work with enchanted targets, but the ones she used were nothing like the ones at Wyndemere. Mack shot at a target that started to dance the moment his fire arrow came near, adding to his frustration.

"My grandfather treats me like I'm still a little kid," he said. "He has so many secrets! After everything I've done—we've done—he doesn't still trust me with the truth." Mack's arrow finally hit the mark, and the target exploded into flames.

Darren shot lightning at another target. This one shrank and then grew and then shrank again until his lightning bolt hit one of the outer rings.

"At least you have someone to talk to," Darren said as he nocked another lightning arrow. "It's really hard keeping secrets from Ray. And for the first time in my life, I can't count on him to help me through this Changer stuff. I'm alone."

"I hadn't thought about it that way," Mack said. "I guess I've sort of taken it for granted, but that's probably because my grandfather can only talk about *some* Changer things." Mack leaped into the air and shot at a target on the floor, watching it explode when his fire arrow pierced it. "I've been going crazy these past few months. They tell us about the prophecy, that we're going to lead the Changer nation, and then nada for— what, three months? What's that about?" He landed on his feet and then spun around to shoot at a target that had come up behind them. "How can you just tell us that and then walk away?"

Darren agreed. Mack's frustration was feeding his own. Instead of making themselves feel better, blowing off steam in target practice was just making them both angrier.

"Well, now I've got a stupid curse on top of everything else," Darren said, turning to shoot a lightning arrow at a target that had circled around them. "If someone in my family *does* have Changer powers, I'll have to break the curse to find out. And, for real, how am I gonna find the spider who cast a curse on my ancestor thousands of years ago?"

"It's crazy," Mack said, shaking his head. "And even if my grandfather could help you, I can practically guarantee he wouldn't. He'd make you figure it all out on your own—like it's part of your own special *journey*. He won't tell me a thing about that golden *kitsune* I saw on the battlefield, and I saw her *again* today."

The *naga* who had been practicing with water arrows on the other side of the arena stopped what she was doing and jogged over to them. "Did you say 'golden kitsune'?" she asked.

Mack and Darren froze for a minute. They hadn't realized they were talking loud enough for her to hear them. The prophecy was a secret—the First Four had told them to keep it to themselves, for now. Had she heard that, too?

"Sorry—I'm Nicole," she said. "From New York."

"I'm Mack, and this is Darren . . . What exactly did you hear?" he asked. "Or should I say, what did you listen in on?"

Nicole stepped back with an angry expression. "I wasn't listening on purpose," she said. "It was impossible not to hear you—you were yelling."

"We're sorry," Darren said quickly. "It's just that we were discussing something private."

"I only heard the words 'golden kitsune,'" Nicole said, softening a bit. "And I didn't mean to eavesdrop." She spun on her heel and started to walk away.

"Wait—do you know anything about a golden kitsune?" Mack asked. "It's really important. I'm sorry I was a jerk."

"It's okay," Nicole said, coming back. "I was just surprised that you guys didn't know about her. She's like the Changers' boogeyman, half myth, half superscary history."

Mack took a breath so he wouldn't sound too impatient and send her away again. "Can you tell us what you know?"

"Well, there's not all that much to tell. When I was little, my grandmother used to say the Shadow Fox would get me if I wasn't good. I guess she was real once—a few hundred years ago, she was a *kitsune* named Sakura, and she had a special ability. She was a memory eater."

"A memory eater? What's that?" Mack asked.

"A memory eater can consume whatever memories it wants—suck them right out of your brain! When Sakura did that—ate memories—she also ate Changer powers. They became hers."

Darren was intrigued. Borrowing powers was something Mack could do. "I thought *kitsunes*—at least powerful ones—could all borrow other Changers' powers," he said.

"*Borrow*," Nicole said with a nod. "Sakura didn't borrow. She *stole*. Apparently, she was able to keep the powers permanently. The Changers she took them from lost both their memories and their Changer gifts . . . forever."

"And her name was Sakura?" Mack asked.

"That's what my grandmother told me," Nicole answered. "In the 1600s, I guess Sakura used her abilities to cause a lot of trouble, at least until the First Four took her down."

"What kind of trouble?" Darren asked.

"She hunted down the Changers who were on the side of the First Four. She ate their memories and stole their powers until she became really strong. Then she turned a bunch of Changers against the First Four and the Changer nation," Nicole answered.

Mack was still dumbfounded that a *kitsune* could be so evil—evil enough to start a rebellion. Changers were supposed to stick together—the First Four had always told them that. "And she was golden? Why was she called 'the Shadow Fox'?"

"That's the really spooky thing," Nicole continued.

"My grandmother said that she only appeared golden to the people she was hunting. To everyone else she looked almost like a shadow, with jet-black fur and dark, shadowy flames around her paws. That's why they called her 'the Shadow Fox.'"

Mack's eyes widened. If that was true, then he was being hunted—by one of Jiichan's former students. An evil *kitsune* who wanted to turn the Changers against the First Four.

Why is she after me? he wondered. *I need to find out more about her, quickly.*

Maybe Jiichan wasn't going to tell him what he needed to know, but Mack knew one person who was an expert at uncovering old secrets in even older books—Fiona.

"Uh, thanks, Nicole," he said, signaling Darren. "We have to go, but we'll catch you later."

"No problem," she said. With that, she lifted her water bow and shot another liquid arrow at a flaming target, putting it out.

"We should find Fiona and Gabriella," Mack said to Darren. "This could get serious."

Darren pulled out his phone and sent a group text to the two of them:

> Need to meet. Mack's with me.

A second later, Fiona texted back:

> At the library. Meet me here.

Another second after that, Gabriella chimed in:

> Finishing up at the arena. On my way.

Fiona sat at a table in the middle of the library, surrounded by books. Mack and Darren joined her, and moments later, Gabriella arrived.

Mack told them about seeing the golden *kitsune* and following her into the forest. Then Darren filled Fiona and Gabriella in on what they had learned from Nicole.

"It didn't seem like she was hunting me," Mack said. "She said she had a message, like she just wanted to talk. But if this *kitsune* really is hunting me, I need to know why. And I need to know how to protect myself. My grandfather won't tell me anything."

"Are you sure there was nothing about her in *The Compendium*?" Gabriella asked Fiona.

Fiona nodded. "I looked and looked. There was

nothing there—unless she's so secret *The Compendium* doesn't want us to know about her. I guess that's possible." She looked around the library. "There might be something here. This library is full of enchanted books. One of them has to have some information about Sakura." Her eyes lit up with excitement when she scanned the shelves, Mack's problems temporarily forgotten.

"But which one?" Mack asked. "It could take years to find the right book."

"Not if you know who to ask," Fiona said with a smile. She walked over to the reference librarian's desk.

Darren wasn't surprised that the librarian already knew Fiona by name. He heard his friend ask for books about evil Changers. "For research," Fiona said a little sheepishly.

"I think I have exactly what you need," the librarian answered. "Come with me."

Fiona waved the others to join her, and they followed the librarian deep into the stacks. The librarian pulled a thick old book from a shelf. "*Bad Blood: A History of Malevolent Changers*," she said.

Fiona thanked her, and the four Willow Cove Changers sat at a table in the back of the library, where they couldn't be overheard.

Mack waited impatiently while Fiona searched the index for the words "Sakura," and "Shadow Fox." "Is there a section on *kitsune*?" he asked.

Fiona shook her head. "I think this book is like *The Compendium*. The words kind of dance on the page. I'm not sure it wants me to read it."

"Oh, great," Mack said sarcastically. "The book is going to keep secrets from me too."

Fiona leafed through the pages and then closed the book with a sigh. "I'm sorry, the words keep moving, and even if they settled down, I think they're in another language."

"Maybe there's another book," Mack said, scanning the shelf that volume had come from. "I'm getting desperate here."

"Maybe *you* have to read it, Mack," Gabriella began. "Remember when *The Compendium* only let me read the passage about the Ring of Tezcatlipoca? The information could only be read by those of Aztec blood."

Fiona handed the book to Mack, and he opened it to a random page. After a minute, the words rearranged themselves, and a title appeared on the top of the page: "The Shadow Fox."

"Wow," Fiona whispered, reading over his shoulder. "There's a whole section on a *kitsune* named Sakura Hiyamoto."

"That must be her!" Darren exclaimed, moving to look at the book as Mack read.

"'Sakura, also known as the Shadow Fox. A former student of Mr. Akira Kimura, First Four, Class A, nine-tailed *kitsune*. A rare evil *kitsune*, the Shadow Fox gains power by eating the memories and absorbing the powers of other Changers, leaving them helpless. She was active in the late 1600s, when she formed a rogue band that nearly tore the Changer nation apart. The First Four were able to arrest and imprison her comrades, but Sakura's ability to eat memories made capturing her a challenge, and she eventually went into hiding. She hasn't surfaced in many years. Her whereabouts remain unknown.'"

The rest of the entry confirmed what Mack had

already learned from Nicole—that the Shadow Fox appeared golden only to those who she hunted.

"I can't believe she was your grandfather's student," Fiona said. "What could have made her go so bad?"

"I don't know," Mack said. "I've been trying to find out from Jiichan ever since Sefu mentioned it, but he won't tell me."

"Are you absolutely sure she was golden when you saw her?" Fiona asked.

Mack nodded, his expression fierce. "Which means she's hunting me, and I'm going to find out why."

"You can't!" Gabriella said, throwing Mack an incredulous look. "That's way too dangerous."

"If she's hunting you, and you go after her, you'll be giving her exactly what she wants," Darren said. "And we don't know how her power works. She could knock you out before you even have a chance to fight."

"You'll lose your powers," Fiona added.

"Look, I may never see her again," Mack said, brushing off their concerns. "It's been months between sightings. But I'm tired of waiting around for the scraps of information my grandfather is willing to feed me.

This *kitsune* wants something from me—she even said she has a message for me—and I need answers from her."

"Maybe your grandfather will tell you more now that you've seen her again," Gabriella said.

Mack shook his head. "It's hopeless. He still thinks of me as a little kid. If I tell him I've seen the Shadow Fox again, he might even force us all to go home . . . to cancel the Youngling Games. I can handle this on my own."

"No, Mack," Darren said firmly. "You've taken some risks before, but this is too much. You know I'm as frustrated with the First Four's secrets as anyone else, but we're in over our heads here. You have to promise us you won't go after her."

"Or at least . . . if you see her again, take me with you," Fiona added. "I'm protected from mind control spells because I know the Queen's Song. I can protect you if things go bad."

Mack chewed on his lip, deep in thought. *We've faced much worse threats than this and come out okay. I don't know why they're so worried. The Shadow Fox has gotten past all of* the First Four's protections already, so if she really does have a message for me, she's going to deliver it no matter what. I'd rather face her head on and hear what she has to say; that way I have the upper hand.

But Mack didn't say any of that out loud. Instead, he smiled up at his friends and agreed. He didn't want them to worry . . . or to try and stop him.

"Don't worry. I won't go after her alone."

Chapter 9
THE YOUNGLING GAMES

The next day Gabriella spent most of her time hanging out with her new friends and exploring the parts of the Wyndemere campus she hadn't seen the day before. She also checked out some of her competitors, who were in the arena to train on the agility and enchanted hurdles courses. They were fast, especially one *bultungin*, but Gabriella knew she was faster. She felt confident about winning. She was so confident, in fact, that she didn't run through the courses again.

Why let the other Changers know just how fast I am before the race? she thought. *I'll let them see what they're up against when the starting buzzer goes off.*

With just an hour to go before the games' opening ceremony, she decided to squeeze in one last warm-up run. The gym and the arena were filled with competitors who had had the same idea, so she headed to the lagoon for a solitary run.

She had made it about halfway around the lagoon when she saw a young woman and an older man in a guard's uniform up ahead on the path. They were obviously having a very heated discussion. Gabriella planned to ignore them and focus on her warm-up, but her ears picked up the words "Shadow Fox," and she reduced her speed to a slow jog to hear more.

The pair was so intent on their argument that they didn't even notice Gabriella.

"You have to cancel. The games aren't safe," the young woman said. She sounded frustrated, as if she had been trying to get through to this guy for a while.

His stony face read that he was just as determined not to listen.

"My team had direct orders from the First Four to track the Shadow Fox," she said. "We had sightings in Willow Cove, and then she disappeared. So we knew she was on the move, but we didn't know where she was going. I lost her for a couple of days, but this morning I picked up her trail again, and it led here. There are *kitsune* paw prints burned all over the forest. She's somewhere around the school."

"Yeah, and there are also *kitsune* students and professors on campus. I even caught a *kitsune* youngling sneaking around here yesterday. We can't cancel the games just because you think you picked up her trail. No one else has seen her, and we have Class B guards posted all over the place. Security isn't taking any risks," the man responded. "Besides, too many younglings and their trainers have traveled here for us to cancel the games based on your *guess*. I'm not risking my neck to report this."

The woman's eyes flashed with anger. "Are you kidding? It's not a guess. She's here, and you're putting all those younglings—the whole school—in danger. You know what the Shadow Fox is capable of."

The man dismissed her concerns. "All I know are the boogeyman stories I was told as a kid. Like I said, we have Class B guards posted at every entrance. Mr. Kimura's enchantments are in place. You're overreacting. I don't know what you saw, but it wasn't the Shadow Fox."

"I am *not* overreacting!" the woman shouted. "At least talk to the headmaster before you go on with the games. Tell her what I found. Let her decide."

The man shook his head. "Go tell her yourself."

"They're already being seated for the opening ceremony. I need Class B credentials to reach her in time."

"Then tell your story to someone else. I'm not going to bother the headmaster with this. What would the Shadow Fox want with a bunch of younglings anyway? If she's after anyone, it's Akira Kimura. But she'd never risk going after him in such a public setting. She'd be apprehended instantly."

Gabriella gave up pretending to jog and came to a dead stop. The Shadow Fox was after Mr. Kimura specifically—not the First Four as a whole? That was new. If she had some kind of vendetta against Mr. Kimura, then . . . was the Shadow Fox trying to use Mack to get to him?

The pair noticed Gabriella then, and moved away, lowering their voices.

Gabriella had heard enough. She had to update the group, in case the woman's warning was true. She ran her hands over her pockets and only then remembered that she had left her cell phone in her dorm room.

She sped back to campus, scanning the crowd on the lawn for signs of Mack, Darren, Fiona, or any of the First Four. The door to the boys' dorm was locked. It wouldn't have mattered, anyway. She didn't even know Mack's room number.

The girls' dorm was empty. *Everyone must already be at the opening ceremony,* Gabriella thought. She took the stairs three at a time, her footsteps echoing in the empty halls, and grabbed her phone from the nightstand next to her bed. She quickly called Fiona, only to find out Fiona's phone went straight to voice mail. She must have turned it off.

Duh, she thought. *Fiona would be going to the lagoon after the opening ceremony. Of course she would turn her phone off.*

Next she texted the group:

> The Shadow Fox is back. She wants to use Mack to get to Mr. Kimura. Find the First Four. Be safe!!!!!

She anxiously waited for an answer, but none came. *They must not have their phones either. I'll have to go and find them in the arena.*

Gabriella knew she could run much faster in her jaguar form. She Changed and raced across the now-empty campus to the arena. When she arrived, she transformed again, just as the opening ceremony was about to start. She scanned the crowd, looking for the First Four, but she couldn't see them in the sea of people. Did they know? Maybe they were already making plans to keep Mack and the campus safe.

The band struck the first notes of their opening number.

"Hey, sit down!" someone behind Gabriella shouted. "I can't see."

Reluctantly, she climbed up to the middle of the arena and took a seat, continuing to search the crowd for Fiona, Mack, and Darren.

The band marched into the arena, and everyone cheered, clapping and whistling. Then the First Four entered the stadium and were met with even louder cheers. Gabriella hadn't realized until now just how beloved the First Four were in the Changer world. This was the first time she'd ever seen them with a big group. She stood and started to make her way toward them, but once again, she was asked to sit down. Wyndemere Academy professors surrounded them. It seemed pretty unlikely that she would be able to get close enough to talk to them, anyway.

The First Four climbed the bleachers to a box that overlooked the entire arena. The man from the argument by the lagoon was already there, but Gabriella didn't see the woman anywhere. Was the guard keeping her away from the First Four?

I *wonder if the First Four even know that she tracked the Shadow Fox to campus?*

"We're very excited to be here to celebrate Wyndemere Academy and the Youngling Games," Mr. Kimura said, his face crinkling into a proud smile. "All of you—athletes and students alike—represent the best our Changer nation has to offer, and our hope for the future. Let's use these games to celebrate peace and friendship for all Changer-kind."

Gabriella only half listened to his words, but the

applause around her signaled that Mack's grandfather had finished his speech.

Next, the entire arena sang the Wyndemere Academy alma mater song, and then Gabriella watched groups march into the arena carrying banners celebrating sports, clubs, and academics at Wyndemere, and welcoming the competitors to campus. Each group stopped to bow to the First Four.

Will I really be one of the First Four one day, sitting in their places with Fiona, Mack, and Darren? Or will the Shadow Fox turn us on one another and bring an end to the prophecy?

A group of ten students ran to the center of the track, and even Gabriella was momentarily thrilled when they all transformed and performed a magical acrobatics act—flying, leaping, and twisting in the air. The crowd went wild, and the games were officially opened.

Gabriella thought about skipping her events to continue the search for her friends. Then she realized they would all find her if she stayed where she was supposed to be—on the track.

She joined the other athletes on the side of the field

for the first race: the enchanted hurdles. She spotted Darren, who was also waiting for his competition. His elemental archery event was next to be held. Mack was in that contest too, and he should have been on the field getting ready.

He wasn't.

"Wasn't that cool? Did you see—" Darren asked, pointing to the acrobats leaving the field.

Gabriella shook her head. There wasn't time to talk about the ceremonies. "Have you seen Mack?" she asked, cutting him off. "I think he might be in danger."

"Danger?" Darren asked, lowering his voice. "Did you see—"

Gabriella leaned in and whispered. "I overheard people—a guard and someone who said she was working for the First Four—talking about the Shadow Fox. She's on campus. And the person the First Four hired said she's after Mr. Kimura."

"Mr. Kimura?" Darren asked. "But she's hunting Mack."

"Exactly," Gabriella said. "What better way to get to Mr. Kimura than through his grandson? And you know Mack—he thinks she wants to talk. Promise or no promise, I'm sure if there's another Shadow Fox sighting, he'll go after her on his own. "

Darren nodded. "I haven't seen Mack since breakfast. He said he wanted to put in some time in at the art studio before the games and disappeared. I hope he didn't hear what you did."

"I'm worried that he's not on the field yet," Gabriella said. "When he gets here, make sure he stays with you. He can't go after the Shadow Fox on his own. And if you see Fiona, let her know what's happening."

"You've got it," Darren said. "And good luck."

"Good luck?"

He pointed to the field, where other Changers were already taking their lanes for the enchanted hurdles.

"Oh, right, I forgot. Thanks," she said.

Gabriella transformed and took her position on the starting line. She heard murmurs from the crowd. Most *nahuals* took the shape of dogs, not jaguars. She knew that black jaguars were both unusual and believed to be very powerful, and Gabriella was about to show them how true that was.

For a moment she pushed aside her worries and enjoyed the admiration, at least until her competitive spirit kicked in. She narrowed her eyes and focused on the track. Enchanted hurdles changed heights, so she had to pay close attention.

The starting buzzer went off, and so did Gabriella. She took the first hurdle easily and then nearly clipped the second with her sharp claws when it jumped to meet her. After that she was in her stride, running and jumping like the champion she was.

Gabriella was used to being far ahead of everyone else on the track, but she had never competed against Changers (other than Mack) before. Halfway through the race she realized that someone was right next to her. She and the other racer were neck and neck. The crowd cheered, urging them on.

Finally, some real competition! Gabriella thought.

The idea gave Gabriella the push she needed. She had never run faster or jumped higher. As she neared the finish line, she reached inside and dug deep for one final burst of speed.

In a flash she took in the faces of the people in the

stands. The noise she heard wasn't cheering—it was screaming.

What is happening?

Gabriella risked a glance at her opponent. She saw a black streak with even darker flames licking at its paws. She wasn't racing another youngling.

Gabriella was racing against the Shadow Fox.

Chapter 10
LOCKDOWN

Fiona could feel the panic building around her as the kids in the stands realized exactly who Gabriella was racing against. It started out as a few scared voices and then rose to a crescendo of shouts. The screams echoed around her as she made her way down the stands toward the track.

Fiona pulled her phone out and turned it on. She had one text from Gabriella just moments before the race:

The Shadow Fox is back. She wants to use Mack to get to Mr. Kimura. Find the First Four. Be safe!!!!!

Fiona gasped.

I have to find Mack and the others, she thought. *We have to keep him from going after the Shadow Fox alone.*

An announcement reverberated over the arena's loudspeakers. "The Youngling Games have been suspended. Evacuate the arena in a calm and orderly fashion. All students and teachers are to report to the castle sublevels immediately. Follow lockdown protocols and await further instructions."

Students were running and tripping over one another in the rush to flee the stadium. Someone grabbed Fiona's arm and tried to pull her toward the castle with him.

"You're going the wrong way!" he shouted.

Fiona shook him off. The boy took off with the rest of the crowd.

"I repeat," the announcer said. "The Youngling Games have been suspended. All students and teachers are to leave the arena in a calm and orderly manner. Report to the castle sublevels immediately. Follow lockdown protocols and await further instructions."

The students pushing past her were anything but calm and orderly.

With chaos all around, Fiona stood quietly for a moment and tried to scan the crowd for where Mack might be. She didn't see him or Darren anywhere, but Gabriella was still in the center of the field. She had come to a standstill beside the Shadow Fox. A jolt of adrenaline shot through her. She needed to get down there.

Fiona couldn't get a good look at her friend with all the people swarming past. She pushed her way through the crowd to get to Gabriella before the Shadow Fox could do any harm. Fiona fought against the river of people rushing in the opposite direction. She got knocked down twice and could already feel the bruises forming on her arms when she finally had a clean line of sight.

Gabriella hadn't moved. Her eyes were still locked on the Shadow Fox's. Was the Shadow Fox already stealing her friend's memories?

Fiona dashed toward Gabriella. Out of the corner of her eye, she saw a red streak. Is *that* Mack?

The streak was gone as soon as she saw it, but Fiona started singing a protection song her mother had taught her. She hoped it would be strong enough to keep both Mack and Gabriella, as well as herself, safe from the Shadow Fox.

She reached Gabriella's side and had barely sung three notes before Sefu leaped onto the field in his *bultungin* form, taking a stand between the girls and the *kitsune*.

The Shadow Fox grinned and bounded away, shadowy flames licking at her paws. Sefu gave chase.

"Are you all right?" Fiona asked.

Gabriella transformed. "I'm fine," she said. "I don't think she was going to hurt me. It was like she was playing with me. She just wanted to make sure that everyone knew she was here or at least . . . make sure Mack knew she was here."

"I saw her expression before she ran off," Fiona said with a shudder. "It was like the screams and the panic were making her *happy*."

"Have you seen Mack?" Gabriella asked, looking around.

"I think I saw him a minute ago," Fiona said. "He had Changed, so look for something red."

They searched the crowd, but neither girl spotted Mack. Darren, Ms. Therian, and Yara ran toward them with Mr. Kimura right on their heels.

"Where's Makoto?" Mr. Kimura asked.

"I think he was here a minute ago," Fiona answered, "but I lost him in the crowd."

"Have you seen him?" he asked Darren.

Darren shook his head. He exchanged an uneasy glance with Fiona and Gabriella. They all knew Mack would follow the Shadow Fox and confront her if he got the chance.

Mr. Kimura looked as if he was about to give them some orders, but Ms. Therian spoke first.

"Go and look for your grandson in the castle, Akira. She's after you and Makoto," she said. "The rest of us are safe for now."

The sound of Ms. Therian's voice, filled with concern, sent a shiver up Fiona's spine. She watched her teacher Change into a werewolf.

"Take the younglings with you, Akira," Yara said gently. "Dorina and I will search for the Shadow Fox."

Yara, a water Changer like Fiona, couldn't Change

on land, but she still had incredible powers in her human form. She climbed onto Ms. Therian's back and took hold of her thick fur. They galloped off into the gathering darkness.

"Come, children," Mr. Kimura said, trying to keep the worry out of his tone. "Quickly. Quickly."

It was eerie how fast the arena had emptied. Trampled banners littered the track. Some kids had left behind sweatshirts, backpacks, books, and even phones in the desperate panic to get away.

The small group ran across campus to the castle and headed downstairs to the basement, following the low rumble of frightened voices. Student monitors and guards stood at all the exits, keeping an eye on anything or anyone that moved. The basement, which would have seemed huge at any other time, looked small now that it was packed with kids.

Mr. Kimura motioned for Fiona, Gabriella, and Darren to join the other students and then stood quietly at the main entrance, his eyes taking in every corner of the room.

One by one, as the groups of students spotted the

leader of the First Four, they whispered to one another to be quiet. In minutes, there was total silence.

"Has anyone seen my grandson, Makoto? He goes by the name of Mack."

He was met by blank stares.

"He's a *kitsune*, red fur, with two tails," Mr. Kimura said.

There were a lot of shaking heads. No one volunteered an answer.

"You stay here," Mr. Kimura said to the three Willow Cove Changers. "Don't leave under any circumstances. I need to get somewhere quiet so I can meditate and search for Makoto."

Fiona watched a disappointed and clearly frightened Mr. Kimura leave the room.

Soon the basement was a cacophony of noise again as the students began an excited recounting of the day's events with claims about who had seen the Shadow Fox first and how quickly they had managed to leave the stadium. The most frightened of them were subjected to some good-natured teasing now that everyone was safe within the castle walls.

Fiona, Darren, and Gabriella sat quietly with a group of high schoolers, too worried about Mack to join in on the chatter.

Then the teens noticed who Gabriella was.

"Hey, aren't you the *nahual* the Shadow Fox was chasing?" one girl asked.

"I don't think she was chasing me. It was more like she was making sure we all knew she was here. And besides," Gabriella added with a slight grin, "I was winning."

The boy next to her leaned in. "Did you lose any memories?"

"I don't think so," Gabriella said.

Fiona could tell that the kids were all waiting for some juicy gossip. "If the Shadow Fox had stolen any of her memories, there's no way Gabriella would *remember* losing them," she pointed out.

"I heard he's after Mr. Kimura's grandson, the *kitsune*," another guy said. "There are rumors that the grandson is being groomed to be one of the new leaders. Did he say anything to the three of you? We saw you come in with him on Thursday."

Fiona shook her head. "Not a word," she said.

"Can you imagine if the Shadow Fox gets her hands on him?" the guy continued. "There will be a civil war for sure."

"What?" Darren asked. "Why a civil war?"

"Yeah, what do you mean?" Fiona asked. Dread was building in her stomach. It seemed pretty clear to her now that the Shadow Fox wanted to harm Mack and Mr. Kimura, and probably the rest of the First Four. But a civil war was much bigger than that.

"Isn't it obvious?" the first girl asked.

"Not to us," Gabriella answered with an edge to her voice. She thought she'd left mean girls behind when she became a Changer, but apparently Wyndemere had its own share of them.

"Oh, sorry," the girl said quickly. "I forgot you were younglings and haven't sat through all the Changer history courses we have."

One of the other girls stepped up to explain. "All the Shadow Fox has to do is steal the happy memories you have of your friends to turn you against them. That's what she did last time. The Changer nation was on the edge of a civil war when the First Four brought her and her followers down."

Gabriella shook her head. "So what? How is taking him going to start a civil war?"

Fiona felt the color draining from her face as she put the pieces together. "If Mack is destined to be one of the new First Four, then people will follow him. Maybe even into Sakura's army."

"And if she's able to eat our memories too—" Darren continued.

"Then she could brainwash us into doing whatever she wanted. Even destroying the Changer nation that we've been charged to protect," Fiona finished.

"So she doesn't want to hurt Mack—she wants to use him to start a war?" Gabriella asked, turning back to the group.

The kids around her all nodded. "That's what she did last time," they said.

Fiona eyed her friends uneasily. If Sakura got her hands on Mack, she'd turn him against *them*. Could she fight her friend if she had to? Fiona didn't think she could.

She motioned for Gabriella and Darren to join her in a quieter corner.

"Mack has no idea what he's up against," she said. "He thinks he's looking for answers, but he's walking into a trap. And even if the guards or First Four find Mack, Sakura could just eat their memories too. There's no other way. . . . I'm going to try to find him."

"It's too risky," Darren said. "You'll be in just as much danger as Mack is. Maybe even more. She'll keep Mack safe to get at his grandfather, but who knows what she might do to you!"

"I have to try," Fiona answered. She scanned the room, looking for an exit that wasn't as heavily guarded as the others.

"We're coming with you," Gabriella said. "You can't go alone."

"No!" Fiona said in a fierce whisper.

She looked around to make sure no one was listening. The last thing she needed right now was for people to find out her mother was queen of the *selkies*. They were already scared. Fiona was sure they'd turn on her just as Jess and Mindy had in the cafeteria. "I can protect myself with the Queen's Song, remember? It's a defense against mind control spells, which—I'm guessing—includes memory eating. But I don't know if I can protect you, too. You have to stay here."

Gabriella started to argue, but Fiona cut her off. "You know I'm right," she insisted.

Grudgingly, Gabriella and Darren agreed.

Gabriella squeezed her friend's shoulder. "Please be supercareful," she said. "And come back with Mack, safe and sound."

"I'll do my best. Now distract that student monitor so I can slip out."

Moments later, while Gabriella and Darren quizzed the monitor about the history of the school, Fiona darted behind them and slipped out the doorway seemingly unnoticed.

The hall was dark and empty. Luckily, Fiona's *selkie* eyes could see pretty well in the darkness, even when she was in human form.

She had a pretty good idea where Mack would have gone to confront the Shadow Fox. The woods and the castle would be full of guards seeking the evil *kitsune*.

But there was one place on campus that would be empty, the one place they were told not to go: the northeast tower of the castle.

Fiona set out in search of it.

Chapter II
THE NORTHEAST TOWER

Mack sat in the stands and watched as a seven-tailed *kitsune* raced with Gabriella. He saw the *kitsune* as golden, with orange and yellow flames licking at her paws, but he could tell by the screams around him that everyone else saw the Shadow Fox.

According to the book they'd read, the fact that Mack saw her as golden meant he was being hunted, but his interaction with Sakura didn't seem that way. She said that she wanted to talk—she had something she needed to tell him.

I know it would be smarter to hide, he thought. *But this is my only chance to find out what she has to say. I'll never get her message unless I go after her now.*

Mack was halfway up the stadium, in the middle of a huge crowd, and yet Sakura seemed to know exactly where he was. As the race came to a stop, she turned to look at him square in the face before turning her eyes back on Gabriella with a sly grin.

Gabriella held the *kitsune*'s stare. She didn't look frightened. She looked fierce.

As if in a trance, Mack started to make his way down the bleachers, Changing so that he could move faster. He saw Fiona make her way toward Gabriella and then saw Sefu Change and jump between them and the Shadow Fox. Sakura flicked her eyes at Mack and disappeared.

Sefu stared after her, but she had already vanished in a fog of golden smoke.

Sakura was signaling him to follow. Mack could feel it. Well, he was going to turn the tables on her. He set off in the same direction he thought she had taken across the lawn.

The hunted was about to become the hunter.

In the chaos and confusion of the arena, Mack was able to slip out before anyone saw him. He was at the gates when he heard the announcement that the games were suspended and that everyone had to report to the castle's basement. He had to be fast, or he'd be surrounded by a stampede of frightened kids. And he had to avoid the student monitors that would be making sure everyone did as they were told.

He sped across the campus. His first instinct was to search in the forest, where he had seen Sakura before. He stepped into the woods and saw guards everywhere. If Sakura was really hiding out in the forest, there was no way Mack would be able to get to her before being stopped by security.

She was too smart for that. She wanted Mack to find her, and she wanted to make sure they could talk alone. But where could that be? The entire campus was filled with guards.

Then he remembered—the northeast tower!

The northeast tower was the one place they were told to stay away from, which made it the very best place to hide. There would be fewer guards patrolling that area since the entries were blocked off and no one was supposed to be there.

The first floor of the castle was empty except for a few student monitors. It seemed everyone else had already made their way to the basement for safety. Mack quickly crept down the hall toward the northeast tower, staying as close to the wall as he could. Halfway there, he had to slip into the game room and hide behind the door as a panicked monitor dashed down the hall, yelling to the kitchen staff to begin lockdown procedures.

I wish I knew a good illusion spell, he thought. Illusion was a *kitsune* power that Mack hadn't yet mastered. He made a mental note to start working on it when they got back to Willow Cove.

Mack crept up the stairs to the second floor. The hall leading to the tower was dark and deserted, littered with ladders and power tools. He raced to a door at the end of the corridor, which was hanging slightly ajar, the chain across it unlocked. From the doorway, Mack thought he could smell char.

She's inside!

He transformed back into his human form as a gesture of peace. Sakura might immediately go into battle mode if she saw him as a *kitsune*, but two people could talk to each other, right?

He stepped through the doorway, closing the door behind him quietly so no one would think to search there. The entranceway to the tower was dark and dusty. The floorboards creaked beneath his feet. A few areas were roped off with construction tape, but behind the tape he could see that this tower was mostly used for storage. He crept from room to room, finding strange, enchanted objects. Most were covered in plastic sheets to protect them from the construction dust and paint, and he didn't recognize those that weren't. But they all shimmered with magic.

Mack summoned a fireball to help light the way. It had grown dark outside, and there were no lights that Mack could find in the tower. A full moon shone through the narrow windows, giving all the sheet-covered objects an eerie glow—except in the next room.

It was as if the room itself swallowed light. Mack could barely make out the shape of the objects inside, but he guessed that they had been used for dark magic.

Instead of a magical shimmer, a kind of shadow swirled around them.

He peered around the edges of the room to make sure that Sakura wasn't hiding in there with him and then made his way up a spiral staircase to the tower's next level. Each level he explored had rooms filled with dusty objects, but none showed signs of the Shadow Fox.

Slowly and carefully, checking the room on each level, he made his way to the top. He was about to give up on finding her when he pushed his way through a trapdoor to climb into the room at the very top of the tower. He left the trapdoor open, in case he had to make a quick getaway. Then he turned in a circle, searching for Sakura, but the room was empty. He was both relieved and angry.

It must have been guards patrolling the tower who unlocked the chain, not Sakura. I should have stayed in the forest, he thought. *I've wasted all this time, and now I won't be able to find her.*

He had just started to walk back to the trapdoor when a shadow began to pulse around it, like the dark magic that surrounded the objects he found in that one room.

The shadow of a cloaked figure loomed larger as it filled the opening and reached the room's ceiling.

The trapdoor closed with a bang, and the shadow moved toward him.

Mack backed into the wall and took a defensive position that the *nykur* professor had taught him just yesterday. His eyes darted from window to window. Each was nothing more than a narrow slit, but he'd be able to slip through if he had to. But there was one big problem—he was hundreds of feet in the air, and he'd fall straight to his death. Some *kitsunes* like his grandfather had the ability to fly, but Mack hadn't developed that particular power yet. He realized in an instant how woefully unprepared he was to face his grandfather's enemy—how much training still lay ahead of him.

Mack was about to be swallowed up by whatever this dark shadow was. He felt young and small—how foolish he had been to think he could confront his grandfather's strongest enemy on his own and emerge unscathed.

A sob caught in his throat.

Jiichan, he thought. I *was wrong. I'm so sorry.*

Chapter 12
Sakura

Mack's whole body trembled as the shadow reached out and began to engulf him. He closed his eyes tight. He didn't want to see what was coming toward him. But then he felt the darkness pulsing around him. It wasn't swallowing him up. It was *embracing* him.

Mack opened his eyes.

The shadow drew back and swirled before turning into a human. A beautiful woman wearing a long hooded cloak stood before him. "Please don't be afraid," she said.

The woman's voice immediately put Mack at ease. In fact, everything about her made him feel safe.

Mack almost laughed at how scared he had been a

minute before. This woman couldn't be evil. She was enchantingly beautiful, and her warm air had a calming effect on him. Like Mack, she had pale skin and dark eyes. Her black hair, straight like his, cascaded to her waist.

"I'm glad to finally meet you, Mack. I'm Sakura." She sat on a window ledge and patted the ledge next to her. "Come. Sit beside me so we can get to know each other."

A whisper of worry entered Mack's heart. *Beautiful or not, she's supposed to be dangerous.* He shook his head. "I'll stay where I am," he said.

Though, Mack thought, *I have no idea if I'm any safer standing across the room. The book from the library never explained how her powers work; could she get my memories from all the way over here?*

Sakura smiled, as if she could hear his anxious thoughts. "There's nothing to be afraid of. I only want to talk. You can leave any time you want," she said, waving toward the trapdoor.

Mack half expected it to open with the wave of her hand, but it remained closed.

"There is something I want to talk to you about," she said. "I hope you'll give me a chance."

"Go on," Mack said. "But I'm not coming any closer."

She nodded. "As you wish."

"So what is it? What have you been trying to tell me?" he asked, pretending to be braver than he felt.

"War is coming," she said, gazing out the window to the grounds below. "One that will divide the Changer nation." Her voice didn't match her message. She might have been telling him that she was about to serve cake and ice cream; it was so sweet and soothing.

Mack didn't say anything. And he didn't take his eyes off her face.

"You will be one of the new leaders," she said. "You'll have to choose between a life looking backward, as your grandfather and the rest of First Four do, or one that looks forward, as I have."

"My grandfather and the rest of the First Four don't trust you. In fact, my grandfather is so freaked out about what happened when you were his student that he won't even talk to me about it."

She shook her head with a sad smile. "They've misled you. I frightened them because I was willing to face the future. They are rooted in the past."

"The book in the library said you were dangerous and power hungry. That you tried to start a war."

"More lies," she said. "Every book has a writer, and writers choose sides. I don't want war—no one wants that. But if the Changers are going to survive, we need a revolution. It's looming over us, can't you feel it?"

"I haven't heard anything about a war or a revolution," Mack said.

"Each and every day, the Changers grow increasingly tired of the First Four's rule. It's just a matter of time before all this"—she gestured toward the rest of castle—"comes tumbling down."

"Are you trying to tell me that there are a bunch of Changers—your *followers*—who are plotting against the First Four?" Mack asked. "Why haven't we seen them?"

"They are hidden right in your midst. Like me, they're done with the First Four's world of duty and responsibility." She said the words as if they were curses. "They've become so wrapped up in protecting humans that they've forgotten about where their first loyalty lies. Why did Circe awaken this magic in us if we're not to use it?"

"They do use it," Mack said defensively. "They use it to help people."

Sakura snickered. Her voice cracked and became less soothing—just for a second. "I don't want to hurt people," she said. "But enough of this blending in with normal humans, hiding our magic. Auden Ironbound saw what was wrong with that, though his logic was flawed. We have to embrace our future. It's time for the Changers to come out of hiding, to show the world who we truly are, and if a few humans are frightened in the process, that's a small price to pay.

"Don't you want to be free, Makoto?" she continued. "Free to stop hiding. Free to use your gifts. Free to live a life filled with magic?"

Mack had to admit to himself that what Sakura said made sense, but that whisper of worry in his heart didn't disappear. In fact, it grew. He thought about his non-magical friends, especially his best friend, Joel. He didn't want Joel to be hurt or scared. That wouldn't be a small price to pay.

"Join us, Mack. Help me lead the Changer nation into the light. Shake off the chains of your grandfather.

Aren't you tired of being treated like a child?"

Sakura's question struck him more than anything she'd said thus far, but he still wasn't ready to drop his guard. "Why me?" Mack asked. "Why not Fiona or Gabriella or Darren?"

"You're the real leader of the group," she crooned. "You're the strongest and the bravest. You have to know that. Make your decision to join us, and your friends will follow. They'll do whatever you tell them to do.

"Come," she said, reaching out to him. "Join me."

For a moment, Mack felt strong and confident in her praise. His hand rose, almost on its own, to clasp hers. Sakura's hands were pale in the moonlight, but her fingernails were long and sharp. They looked like weapons.

At the last minute, Mack drew his hand back and thought about Jiichan. He shook his head. "I have to hear all the facts—not just your side of the story, but the First Four's, too."

Sakura's laugh was light and tinkling. "If your grandfather wasn't so intent on keeping his students in the dark, you'd already have all the facts."

Mack grimaced, thinking about how impatient he often grew when the First Four wouldn't answer his questions.

"I know all about your grandfather's love for secrets," she said. "I was his student too, you know, once upon a time. Why do you think he keeps so many secrets?"

Mack shrugged. He had often wondered the same thing. "He says I'm not ready to know them yet."

Sakura's voice suddenly became harsh and angry. "He wants to *control* you," she said.

Mack shook his head again. Jiichan always said he would reveal his secrets when Mack was ready. And true to his word, he did reveal some, though not quite as quickly as Mack wanted. . . . Could Sakura be right? Did his grandfather want to control him?

"How do you like being *controlled*?" Sakura taunted.

Mack remained silent.

"Would you like to know who your beloved grandfather really is?"

"What do you mean?" Mack asked. Of course he knew who his grandfather was. Still, he didn't stop

Sakura from continuing. He didn't take a step toward the trapdoor.

"When I became your grandfather's student, he was new to teaching. He was arrogant and foolish. He wanted me to master the arts and earn my *kitsune* tails faster than any other. He didn't want that for my benefit," she said. "He wanted it because it would bring fame and glory to *him*."

That didn't make sense to Mack. Jiichan was always trying to get him to slow down, not speed up.

"He pushed me hard—too hard," Sakura said. "I wanted to please him, so I tried my best. But he didn't know, or care, about the risks involved. He had strict standards, and he pushed and he pushed and he pushed."

"B-but you did earn seven tails," Mack stammered. "And you're powerful. Isn't that because my grandfather—"

"Oh, he taught me well," Sakura said, cutting him off. Her voice turned bitter. "But it was about bringing glory to my teacher. He was so intent on himself, on his own fame, that he almost killed me."

"What are you talking about?" Mack asked.

"He wanted me to try a difficult spell—too difficult for a young *kitsune*. The execution of it nearly killed me; I still bear the scars."

"I'm sure he didn't mean it," Mack said. "Jiichan would never put someone in danger to improve his own reputation."

"If that's the case, then why did he swear me to secrecy?"

Mack's forehead wrinkled in confusion.

"The great Akira Kimura wouldn't let anyone know that he was at fault, lest it tarnish his precious reputation. Instead, he blamed me, said that I had tried my hand at dark magic, and banished me from his tutelage." Sakura's voice left all its soothing qualities behind as her anger and bitterness grew.

Mack could feel his own anger growing. It swelled up and erased everything else—all the worry and doubt he was feeling. He thought about every fight he and his grandfather had, until the bitterness erased his love for Jiichan.

Sakura sensed how he was feeling. She flashed

him a triumphant smile. "He's not quite the precious grandfather you knew, is he?"

Mack was silent.

"It's time, Mack. It's time for you to become the leader you truly are. It's time for you join me." She reached out to him again.

This time, Mack took her hand.

Chapter 13
THE SHADOW FOX

Fiona darted through the halls toward the northeast tower, lurking in dark corners to avoid the guards. A couple of times she heard them talking to one another. The concern in their voices was clear. The guards were afraid.

Finally, she slipped into the last hall and made her way to the tower's entrance. The door was closed tight, but not locked. Fiona opened it quietly and crept into a hallway.

The tower was dark, dusty, and quiet. Too quiet. She peered up the spiral staircase and saw dusty footprints on the steps. One set looked like Mack's. The others were dark paw prints that gave off a fiery smell. Sakura!

Fiona dashed up the stairs. She had only gone up one flight when the silence was pierced by a terrible clamor coming from above. The otherworldly sound, kind of a wheezing, sucking screech, rattled her bones and shot fear through her heart. She wanted to run in the other direction, to find the First Four, to get help, but there was no time for that. Mack was in danger. She swallowed her fear and began to sing the Queen's Song—tentatively at first and then more confidently as the words filled her with power and protection. She focused on the dark magic she could sense in the room above.

This ancient piece of *selkie* magic—the most powerful song at her disposal—was one that only those of royal blood could sing. But was it powerful enough to protect both Fiona *and* Mack from the Shadow Fox? She wasn't sure.

The song still on her lips, Fiona burst through the trapdoor leading to the room at very top of the tower. She stumbled, and so did her song when she saw Mack, in his *kitsune* form, limp on the floor. His tails—the powerful tail he had been so proud of earning—were underneath him. His eyes were open, but they stared at nothing, flat and unblinking.

Even worse, the Shadow Fox kneeled over him, biting at his neck.

She's sucking out his memories, Fiona thought. *And his powers, too.*

The Shadow Fox stopped for a moment, and so did the awful noise. The *kitsune* turned to Fiona then, her eyes wide and glittering.

Mack's eyes closed.

Fiona picked up her song again and even tried to hurry through it, hoping that as she came to the end, Mack's protection would be complete and the Shadow Fox would be forced to surrender. But the song held the ancient rhythms of the moon and the tides and could not be rushed.

The Shadow Fox opened her mouth wide, revealing her hyperextended jaws and her three rows of teeth. *You cannot stop me,* selkie *princess,* she sneered. *You've already lost this battle. Join me if you want to be on the right side of this war.*

Fiona shook her head. She kept singing.

The *kitsune's* grin turned to a grimace.

Something's happening! Good magic is getting through! Fiona thought.

She sang louder, holding the evil *kitsune*'s eyes, hoping to keep the Shadow Fox from biting Mack again before help arrived.

The Shadow Fox howled with rage, opening her jaw even wider. She took a step toward Fiona, but Fiona held her ground. The *kitsune* made as if to leap at her, but instead disappeared in a haze of smoke. Fiona thought she heard a deep chuckle as the smoke dissipated.

Kneeling beside Mack, Fiona tried to shake him awake. "Mack, I'm here," she said. "I'm here and you're safe."

He transformed back into his human form, but his eyes remained closed, his body limp. She checked his wrist and found a faint pulse.

She tried to lift him so that she could carry him downstairs to get help, but he was too heavy for her. She didn't want to leave him.

"Help!" Fiona screamed. "Help me!"

No one will hear me all the way up here, she realized. *Everyone's on lockdown in the basement.*

Fiona took a deep breath to calm herself down. She took out her cell phone, but the battery was dead. Could she reach the others telepathically? She had to try. She closed her eyes, concentrating on sending a message to Mr. Kimura and the rest of the First Four.

Mack needs help! she thought.

A second later she heard Mr. Kimura's voice in her head.

Where are you?

In the northeast tower. At the very top. Mack won't wake up. The Shadow Fox was here with him!

Cast a protection spell, Mr. Kimura told her.

Now that she knew help was on the way, Fiona gave in to her tears. They slid down her cheeks as she sang a song of protection, forming a protective bubble around Mack and the tower room.

Seconds later, Mr. Kimura burst through the trap door, followed by Ms. Therian.

"How did this happen," Mr. Kimura said flatly, kneeling at his grandson's side.

Fiona told him everything she knew—about hearing the awful sucking screech and finding the Shadow Fox kneeling over Mack, her sharp teeth in his neck.

"I waited too long to go after him," Fiona said, tears flowing freely now. "I knew he was going to try to find her if he got the chance. He didn't know how dangerous she was. He just wanted to talk to her. Is he going to be okay?"

"He needs to rest." Mr. Kimura sat and cradled Mack's head in his lap.

Ms. Therian crouched beside him and pressed her hand against Mack's neck. A healing light engulfed them. Sakura's teeth marks disappeared, but a set of thin white lines remained. "That's the best I can do," she said. "He might always bear that scar—it's powerful magic."

"I waited too long," Fiona said again. "I'm sorry."

Mr. Kimura shook his head gravely. "Don't blame yourself. I should have put an end to Sakura long ago. This was my doing."

"Mack said she was your student," Fiona said quietly.

"She was," Mr. Kimura said. "My first student. I'm afraid I pushed her too hard. A prophecy had been delivered to me, one that I misinterpreted."

"She craved power, Akira," Ms. Therian said gently.

"The fault is not solely yours. She made her choices long ago."

Mr. Kimura nodded sadly. "When I realized my mistake, I took a step back from our teaching. She wanted to prove herself, to learn more. When I refused, she began looking into dark spells that would increase her power. She wasn't ready, wasn't skilled enough, to cast such spells. One backfired and made her the monster that you saw tonight.

"I knew when Makoto saw her on the battlefield that she was planning to go after him as a way to get her revenge on me," Mr. Kimura continued. "Right before we revealed the prophecy to you, I could sense that Sakura was hiding in Willow Cove, waiting to strike. That's why we sent you here, to the games."

"Sefu, Yara, and Akira were planning to hunt her down in Willow Cove while the four of you were safe on campus," Ms. Therian said quietly. "But just as suddenly as she appeared in Willow Cove, she disappeared again. Now we know she was here all along."

"I knew Mack might try to go after her, but I never thought she'd be able to penetrate the protection spells here," Mr. Kimura said, shaking his head. "She's grown even more powerful since our last encounter six years ago." He smoothed his grandson's forehead. "I'm so sorry, Makoto. I thought I could take care of this before she got near you. You alone have had to bear the burden of too many of my mistakes."

His face was sad and resigned. "The time for keeping secrets is over. We can't leave the children in the dark anymore," he said to Ms. Therian. He turned to Fiona. "I had hoped to keep all of this from you until you were fully trained, but if Sakura is making another bid for power, then it's time that you, Makoto, Gabriella, and Darren are fully immersed in the ways of the Changer nation."

He shook his head again with a bitter laugh. "If I can't keep Wyndemere Academy safe, then perhaps nowhere is safe. You'll have to be ready to face real missions, real involvement, and very real danger."

"We can do it," Fiona said. "You've taught us well. So has Ms. Therian."

"I hope so," he said. "It's time, Dorina."

Ms. Therian got to her feet. "I'll make the arrangements at once."

EPILOGUE

Mack woke up with a start in the middle of the night, rubbing the side of his neck. *Where am I?* he wondered. *And why does my neck hurt?*

His eyes adjusted to the dim light, and he realized he was in some kind of hospital room. Slowly, things started to come back to him—Wyndemere Academy, the Youngling Games, and Sakura.

Sakura!

He remembered the peace he had felt in her presence, and that the peace had turned to worry and then fear and then pain and terror. She had done something to him—something he needed to remember. He searched for the memory but only came up with a dark, shadowy hole where the memory should have been.

I have to remember. I'm going to hurt my friends if I don't. I'm going to do something really, really bad and put everyone in danger.

He looked around and saw his grandfather asleep in the chair at his side, his face creased with worry even in sleep.

Jiichan! It was something to do with Jiichan. Think! Mack told himself, but the memory wouldn't come.

He closed his eyes, and hot tears slid down his cheeks. He was so stupid to go after Sakura on his own. He should have trusted Jiichan more. He shouldn't have been so impatient and so cocky. What Mack had done had somehow helped Sakura, and now the Shadow Fox was going to win.

Win what? He couldn't remember.

Mack wiped his tears and then reached over to wake his grandfather.

He'll know what to do, Mack thought. *He can help me figure out how to fix this.*

Jiichan shook the sleep away and leaned toward Mack with a loving smile.

"Welcome back, Makoto," he said.

Mack opened his mouth to speak—to apologize and to ask for help—but the words that came out were not his own:

"War is coming."

What challenge will the Changers face next?

Here is a sneak peek at

THE HIDDEN WORLD OF Changers

The Spirit Warrior!

Gabriella Rivera rushed out of math class the second the bell rang. She wanted to talk to her friends Fiona Murphy and Darren Smith before their next and final class of the day. It was a class that the rest of Willow Cove Middle School *thought* was an ordinary gym class. Gabriella and her friends alone knew that it was so much more.

Gabriella zigzagged around clusters of other kids, making her way back to her locker. Sometimes, in the midst of her fellow students, it was easy to forget just how different she was from them—just how different everything was. Gabriella had learned on the first day of seventh grade that she was a Changer, someone with the power to transform into a creature the normal world believed was mythological.

In Gabriella's case, she had discovered she was a

nahual, or jaguar, from Aztec mythology. Her aunt and grandmother had always been proud of their Mexican heritage, and they always insisted that the blood of Aztec warriors ran through their veins. Until recently, Gabriella had no idea how true that family story actually was. With her transformation came an array of incredible powers worthy of any warrior—superspeed, sharp claws, and quick reflexes, among other things.

Gabriella caught up with Fiona and Darren near Fiona's locker. Fiona was the secret daughter of the *selkie* queen, a seal Changer who ruled the oceans. Using her *selkie* cloak, Fiona could transform into a seal as well; in her human form she channeled magic into *selkie* songs. Darren's other form was a fearsome bird, an *impundulu*, who could shoot lightning bolts from his razor-sharp talons and create incredible storms. The final member of their group was Makoto "Mack" Kimura.

"Have you seen Mack yet?" Gabriella asked.

Darren shook his head.

"He wasn't in homeroom," Fiona murmured, glancing around to make sure she wouldn't be overheard. "When I called his house last night, his grandfather said Mack would be here for Changers class. The First Four will be here too, so Mack could transform for the first time since . . ." Her voice trailed off.

"Since Sakura bit him," Gabriella said bluntly.

Mack, a huge fan of comic books and superheroes, could transform into a *kitsune*, a magical fox whose paws blazed with fire. Mack could be goofy and more than a bit nerdy at times, but Gabriella liked that he always saw the best in people. When each of his friends, including Gabriella, had trouble controlling their powers, Mack never lost faith in them. He was always the first to say that things were going to work out okay.

Mack's grandfather, Akira Kimura, was also a *kitsune* and one of the First Four—a council of elders who led all the Changers in the world. But even Mack's powerful grandfather couldn't protect him from the Changers' newest enemy, an evil *kitsune* named Sakura Hiyamoto, known to many as the Shadow Fox.

Kitsunes earn tails (up to nine) for accomplishing heroic deeds or learning new skills. One of Sakura's unique abilities was memory eating, which meant that she could consume other Changers' memories and, in doing so, could also absorb their powers. A former student of Mr. Kimura's, she had delved into dark magic, and when that went very, very wrong, Sakura turned on Mr. Kimura. She even started a rebellion against the First Four, and stole powers from many Changers. Her exploits had made her a boogeyman to most young Changers. Sakura had since been hiding from the Changers underground, watching and waiting for her chance to strike. But recently, she had returned and would stop at nothing to have her revenge on Mr. Kimura and the rest of the First Four. That included going after Mr. Kimura's grandson, Mack.

Gabriella and the other young Changers—or younglings, as the Changer world called them—had been back in Willow Cove for only a few days. Over their school's spring break, they had visited Wyndemere Academy, a boarding school for high school–aged Changers. Mack and his friends were supposed to get to know the school and participate in a competition known as the Youngling Games. But Sakura had put a stop to all that, bringing fear and chaos to the Changer world once again.

Sakura had been following Mack for some time, but Mack's grandfather refused to talk to him about her. Frustrated with his grandfather, and determined to get his own answers, Mack followed Sakura and confronted her. Unfortunately, he did so without knowing just how dangerous she could be.

Fiona had saved Mack's life with a *selkie* song—arguably one of the most powerful forms of magic known to Changers—but not before Sakura managed to sink her teeth into their friend. Mack had been unable to tell them what happened and what memories or powers Sakura had stolen from him, but he did know one thing: war was coming. War between Sakura's followers and those who supported the First Four. The First Four were dedicated to protecting humans and Changers alike. Sakura wanted to take the world for Changer-kind alone.

Gabriella shivered thinking about the dark times ahead. Her mother and sister were normal, nonmagical people; so were her soccer teammates and most of her friends. She would do whatever she could to protect them. She hoped to learn more about how to do that and how to defeat Sakura in today's class. And, of course, she also hoped to see Mack.

"Do you think he'll be okay?" Darren asked. "I mean, what if Sakura took his power—like, *stole* it?"

"Mack's our friend, powers or not," Gabriella said. "It's important that we're there for him."

"I wish Mr. Kimura would have let us visit Mack over the weekend," Fiona said. "He was so upset when we saw him last. . . . I'm afraid Mack will think we abandoned him."

"Mack knows we've got his back," Darren said. "The four of us need one another. We're not complete without him. Now let's go so we can tell him that in person."

"There's Mack," Gabriella said as they entered the school's ancillary gym.

Mack and his grandfather were standing in a corner, having a discussion in Japanese. Mr. Kimura had a hand on his grandson's shoulder, as if he was trying to reassure him. Gabriella saw Mack's eyes flick in their direction for a second before he turned his attention back to his grandfather.

He looks different, Gabriella thought. *Guarded.*

Dorina Therian, their primary coach and another member of the First Four, greeted Gabriella and the others. She was the one who had given Gabriella the news that she was a *nahual* the first day of class and then demonstrated her own Changer transformation—into a werewolf.

The other two members of the First Four, Sefu Badawi (a *bultungin*, or hyena Changer) and Yara Moreno (an *encantado*, or dolphin Changer) also waited. They smiled reassuringly at Gabriella and her friends.

Mack and his grandfather finished their talk and joined the group.

"Ready to get this over with?" Mack asked with a queasy smile. "Let's make sure I haven't sprouted a new head or grown an extra row of teeth or . . . lost my powers."

"It's going to be fine," Fiona said. "*You're* going to be fine."

"Of course you are," Gabriella added, giving him a quick hug.

"Yeah, we're here for you no matter what," Darren said.

Mack's queasy smile returned, but he said nothing.

They waited for the First Four to clue them in on what was about to happen.

"I don't want any of you to be frightened," Mr. Kimura said. "Chances are that this is all for nothing, and Makoto will be able to transform without issue. It's important we're together though."

While he was speaking, the other members of the First Four formed a kind of square around Mack. Ms. Therian motioned for Gabriella, Darren, and Fiona to stand a bit farther back, filling in the gaps between their elders.

"Darren, if you would, a force field around all of us for protection might be helpful," Mr. Kimura said.

Darren nodded. Soon, the tips of his fingers were crackling with electricity, forming sparks. While Gabriella watched, those sparks joined together, creating a glowing web. Moments later, the force field encircled all eight of them.

Why would we need a force field if this is just about Mack transforming? Gabriella wondered. *Is Mr. Kimura keeping others out of the circle or making sure Mack can't escape?*

"I'm going to count down, Makoto," Mr. Kimura

said. "When I reach one, you can transform."

Mack nodded, his expression grim.

Gabriella's shoulders tightened as Mr. Kimura began to count from ten to one. Even without thinking she was on the balls of her feet, ready to transform and spring into action if she needed to.

But I won't need to, she thought. *This is only about Mack's transformation.*

Still, she felt her own tension increase with each number. She couldn't imagine what Mack was thinking and feeling. She stared into his face, but his eyes were clouded. With worry? Fear? Anger? She couldn't tell.

"Three, two, one," Mr. Kimura said. He nodded at his grandson.

Gabriella held her breath. Mack transformed, just like she had seen him do so many times before, and he was . . .

Mack! The same as always.

Gabriella exhaled when she saw that her friend had transformed into a fox with sandy-red fur—just like he always had. Orange and yellow flames licked at his paws. Gabriella smiled at him, and Mack seemed to smile back.

But then she saw confusion on the faces of Ms. Therian, Fiona, and Sefu, who were standing behind him.

Mack looked over his shoulder, and when he did, Gabriella saw the cause of their confusion.

Mack had gained a third tail.